G R JORDAN

The Graves of Calgary Bay

A Patrick Smythe Mystery Thriller

First published by Carpetless Publishing 2020

Copyright © 2020 by G R Jordan

All rights reserved. No part of this publication may be reproduced, stored or transmitted in any form or by any means, electronic, mechanical, photocopying, recording, scanning, or otherwise without written permission from the publisher. It is illegal to copy this book, post it to a website, or distribute it by any other means without permission.

This novel is entirely a work of fiction. The names, characters and incidents portrayed in it are the work of the author's imagination. Any resemblance to actual persons, living or dead, events or localities is entirely coincidental.

G R Jordan asserts the moral right to be identified as the author of this work.

G R Jordan has no responsibility for the persistence or accuracy of URLs for external or third-party Internet Websites referred to in this publication and does not guarantee that any content on such Websites is, or will remain, accurate or appropriate.

Designations used by companies to distinguish their products are often claimed as trademarks. All brand names and product names used in this book and on its cover are trade names, service marks, trademarks and registered trademarks of their respective owners. The publishers and the book are not associated with any product or vendor mentioned in this book. None of the companies referenced within the book have endorsed the book.

First edition

ISBN: 978-1-912153-76-3

This book was professionally typeset on Reedsy. Find out more at reedsy.com

Contents

Foreword	v
Acknowledgement	vi
Chapter One	1
Chapter Two	8
Chapter Three	15
Chapter Four	24
Chapter Five	33
Chapter Six	42
Chapter Seven	50
Chapter Eight	59
Chapter Nine	67
Chapter Ten	76
Chapter Eleven	85
Chapter Twelve	95
Chapter Thirteen	101
Chapter Fourteen	109
Chapter Fifteen	117
Chapter Sixteen	126
Chapter Seventeen	133
Chapter Eighteen	141
Chapter Nineteen	149
Chapter Twenty	157
Chapter Twenty-One	161
Chapter Twenty-Two	169
Get Your Patrick Smythe Series Short Story!	174
About the Author	177

Also by G R Jordan

Foreword

This story is set across the varying landscapes of Scotland's west coast. Although set amongst known towns and lochs, note that all persons and specific places are fictional and not to be confused with actual buildings and structures that exist and which have been used as an inspirational canvas on which to tell a completely fictional story.

Acknowledgement

To Susan, Harold, Evelyn, Jean and Rosemary for your work in bringing this novel to completion, your time and effort is deeply appreciated.

"A thing that you see in my pictures is that I was not afraid to fall in love with these people."

Annie Leibovitz

Chapter One

I'm staring at my feet through the tide, before glancing up to the ferry some distance up Loch Ryan. There's a family wrapped up in coats along from me, and they seem to be having fun despite the drizzle coming down. One of the kids even has a bucket with him making sandcastles, probably covering them with the shells picked up from other parts of the beach. He's a chap with a cheeky grin and I watch the father pick him up and spin him around. There are just some days when I think I may be on the wrong path.

But why am I complaining? After all, I have a new business set up in the swish seaside town of Stranraer, a new woman on the scene, and absolutely no cases. This is why I'm sitting on the beach; this is why I'm in such a morbid mood but sometimes I have to remind myself life isn't all that bad.

My mobile is ringing. Answering the call, I hear the tones of my newest recruit, Susan, and she sounds in such a good mood it makes me wonder what the deal is.

'Paddy, I have a lady waiting for you in the office, a Mrs Matheson. She's here to talk to you about her son. Sounds quite serious.'

From the tone of Susan's voice, I can tell the blood is pumping through her. She's only ever worked with me and I nearly got her killed so she thinks that everything about private investigations should be exciting. But she's wrong. Most of the time, I end up hanging around outside houses checking who's going in who shouldn't have gone in, and who's not gone out. Domestic cases can be such a drag.

I tell Susan I'll be back in the office in five minutes and remind her to make the woman a cup of tea. She has an inquisitive mind but sometimes she forgets the base formalities that help make a business run. My mind winds back to *Craigantlet*, my boat currently sitting in the harbour. Normally I would be up the west coast finding my way by instinct and not sitting waiting for the phone call. But these are different days, and I'm afraid my sailing is suffering at the hands of Maggie Calderwood. Not that I'm complaining, because these last weeks have been some of the best of the last years.

Maggie is Susan's mother and after some shenanigans with a bunch of Russian mobsters in Stranraer, I ended up putting her daughter into jeopardy and then rescuing her before starting a relationship with a grateful parent.

As I walk into the office, I can see a well-built woman through the inner glass door, sitting in the chair opposite my desk. She seems agitated and the tea that Susan has made is sitting on my desk untouched. Susan meets me before I go into the rear office, her eyes glazed over with excitement.

'Patrick, her son is dead. We're going to have to find her son's killer.'

'Easy,' I say, before Susan gets too carried away. 'I need to see if we want to take this case. You have no idea what's happened nor any idea who's involved; therefore, you have no idea what the risks are. You can't just go chasing a case—you have to make sure it's not one that's going to get you killed.'

CHAPTER ONE

I open the door of the rear office and the woman's head flicks round immediately. She looks at me with discerning eyes and notices that I do not have a left arm. Following me with her eyes until I sit down behind my desk, she seems agitated. Is there a slight shake to her shoulders? I wonder what caused her to come to me. Sometimes people come out of desperation, sometimes I've been recommended, and sometimes they're here under false pretences.

'Good morning, Madam, my name is Patrick Smythe and I believe you require my services. Simply tell me what has been going on and when you have explained, I'll see if I can help. I believe your name is Matheson?'

I would place the woman somewhere in her sixties, but it looks like it's been a rough life. There are plenty of lines across her face despite the obvious time spent this morning applying her makeup. The worry over her son is obvious.

'I found your advert, Mr Smythe. It said you look into things—things other people are not prepared to. That's why I'm here. I need you to look into the death of my son, Keir. He died three months ago when he was away working on the island of Mull, doing what he thought would be his dream job. You see, he was very caught up with his photography, very into capturing the beauty in this life. Until they found him, on Gometra.'

'Gometra,' I say, my mind racing, thinking about where that is.

'Ulva, it's on the south side of Mull. They found him on the little island, but there's hardly anyone there. The police have looked into the incident and so far, they have nothing. But I need something, something to tell me what happened to him. It's like he doesn't matter anymore, as if we just give it a go and when we find nothing—well, who cares? I want you to care; I want you to tell me what happened to my Keir.'

The woman reaches down into her handbag on her lap, removes a white handkerchief, and begins to dab at her eyes. She's wearing quite a formal suit—a jacket with a blouse and a skirt that reaches to her shins. Her eyes are no longer looking at me; instead, she looks inside her handbag where she slowly draws out a photograph before placing it on my desk.

'I take it this is your son. Is it a recent photograph or just a particular favourite of yours?' That may seem a little harsh, but it is quite important to me. If I am to find her son, I need to know who I'm looking for, not who she thought he was.

'Recent,' she says. 'Taken before he set off on this last adventure. Sometimes I wonder if it was my fault as he was quite a quiet boy, used to stay around the house, even with his photography. But I insisted he needed to get some space away from me, needed to find his own life. And then he died. I need you to tell me why.'

'Okay, Mrs Matheson, why don't you tell me a little more about what he was doing, who he saw, and what actually happened? That way I can see if I can help you.'

'He went to stay with a photographer, a proper one, who lived up near Calgary Bay. He had researched the man and I believe he was quite happy with him. The man is called Jack Doolan and he's reasonably famous for his photography in the area. Keir liked the idea of joining the man, spending some time with him, going here and there over the Island, photographing the birds and whatever else they could find. I know they'd been to Gometra a few times as it was quite remote, but I don't think it was anywhere specific. They went everywhere on Mull.

'I know my son had some friends up there, people he had

CHAPTER ONE

gone out with, but he never mentioned any names. It wasn't really like him. At home, he was always quiet, always one of those stay-at-home kids. It didn't help that his father isn't around anymore, and I think at times he used to get bullied.'

I can tell he is one of those kids looking at the photograph as he has the eyes that don't quite seek you out, don't quite go for you. Instead, he's almost looking away from the camera, afraid someone's going to find him out.

'You indicated he was up there for about three months. Did you see him at all during that time?'

'I only spoke to him on the phone, Mr Smythe, and I received an occasional letter. Keir was always good to his mum, always good at keeping in contact. I don't know if that was because he understood I had only him or whether he needed it. They say you have an instinct as a mother, but that was something I've always struggled with. I didn't really connect with him, didn't really understand him. You'll have to forgive me, Mr Smythe, if I seem a little bit cold at times. My son . . . I've been having difficulty coming to terms with it, spending this time raising him, spending this time making him into a man instead of a . . . mother's boy. And what happens? Somebody just goes and ends it. I need to understand what happened, Mr Smythe. I think you can begin to understand what I'm talking about.'

'You said the police investigated it. How much did they tell you?'

'They said they could find no evidence of anything. They searched the site where he was found; they questioned Mr Doolan; they tried to find out about friends he had. But Keir left the house one night and that was it. Nobody knew where or how or what happened to him. He was found by a local farmer. I guess it's sheep up there. Maybe you don't go much outside on those islands. When I looked it up on the internet, there seemed to be nothing on Gometra. Nothing. I have no idea what he was doing there. I have nothing, Mr Smythe; do you understand me?'

'I take it you do have addresses and contacts of where he was. I need you to write those down. I need you to also get me some more photographs of your son and I require to know whom he corresponded with. If you have a laptop or anything of his, I could do with it as well, with your permission to break into it.'

'He had that all with him, his phone, his tablet; there was none of it at home. The police took it away and I believe they still have it. It might show you photographs because that's what he used it for. I can give you an account to his online storage or photographs, but I can't do a lot more. You see, he's just gone, Mr Smythe . . . like someone just took their finger and thumb and snuffed out the light for no reason. I need to know what happened to him. Do you understand me, Mr Smythe? I have savings. I have the money but tell me what happened to him. Tell me you'll take this case and find out what happened during the last days of my son's life.'

It is best at such times to be unemotional, trying to keep a mind that says, *What are the merits of the case? Why should I take it? Does she have the fee?* Words like these seem to be much more important than any emotional tie. Despite not having a son, I'm finding it difficult to step away. The woman cuts such a sad figure and as I look at her, trying to be neat and tidy in her seat, dressed up as best she can to influence me to take the case, there's an overwhelming swell of pity within me. It's surprising me as much as anyone. But I will certainly take a look. Although given the police have had three months on it and they've told her next to nothing, I'm not sure what I can

CHAPTER ONE

dig up.

I stand up, come around the desk, and shake the woman's hand, telling her that I will look into it for her. I ask if Susan's given her a copy of my rates and fees, to which she simply nods. I ask her to write down anything else she can think of and email it to me, along with those passwords and codes to get into his online storage. With that, I shake her hand, offering my condolences for her loss and advising her I'll do my absolute best to find out what happened.

As soon as Mrs Matheson departs, Susan rushes in from the other office.

'So, are we taking it, Paddy? Are we off to Mull?'

'You could have a little more decorum around her,' I say.

'I didn't say anything when she was here. I was polite, I made her tea, I didn't do anything that was out of line.'

She looks offended and I guess I'm just being cruel for hanging back on my answer.

'Yes, I'm going to take a look at it,' I tell her, 'and you can come up with me but don't get your hopes up. If the police have had these three months, I'm reckoning it's going to be a closed case . . . we'll see what comes.'

And with that, I tell her to start arranging some accommodation and go online myself, to remind myself of the area . . . Gometra. As I recall, it's a very lonely place stuck on the end of a very lonely place—strange place to die. But she never told me how he died, how he was left, where the body was. All I can think of is that it must have been grim because she never even attempted to tell me.

Chapter Two

I have never really taken anyone on a case with me, and Susan is only nineteen, but she is certainly keen. I let her drive the car up to Oban where we take the ferry across to Craignure on what is a rather bleak-looking day. But even given the weather, Mull itself is quite beautiful and I remember doing a little bit of work here before—a bit of work I handed over to the police when things started to get more serious.

But this time as we head up towards Salen on the coast road that lets you look out at the Sound of Mull and the close traffic that passes on the water there, I am getting a sinking feeling that we are not going to be able to find out much. Because our victim was working up near Calgary Bay, Susan managed to book a hotel in Dervaig, but I felt the first thing to do was to go to Gometra. This involves one of the shortest ferry crossings you will ever go on as you head over to the Ulva ferry landing from Oskamull. It is quite strange as you arrive, especially in winter, because there's very few cars about. And when we go over, without our car, we get some strange looks. It will be about a five-mile walk to Gometra, which is as the crow flies, although we will take the road that goes round.

Keir Matheson was found on an old burial site not that far from the more-inhabited areas of Gometra. And when I say more-inhabited, I mean there is a house, but one thing at a time. As we come to the ferry, Susan has a bright smile on her, despite her jeans now being soaked and the heavy drizzle that assaults us. You can smell the sea—all round this island—and part of it makes me long to get back on *Craigantlet*, but I try to keep my head in the game where we are.

Susan has her mobile up, photographing the water between Ulva and the Isle of Mull itself. You can go and visit the Ulva church; you can stay at a B&B on the Ulva island but I'd rather we walk, get to our scene, and then walk back. But this does mean it could be late and the ferry might not run, so I brought a tent.

I thought, at first, Susan would be quite annoyed at this because I wasn't carrying two, but she seems to enjoy the adventure. Although we broke the drive up, I'm still finding it's the afternoon by the time our ferry has crossed.

We stop at the small shop, buying a few provisions. When I say shop, it is more like the tiniest pub on a shore. I look about the concrete jetty where the ferry comes in and there is a couple of tied-up boats and large pink buoys used to secure them when the tide comes in. The ground is rough, grey rock, but there are a few brick cracks and stone defences that keep the pub safe. The great drizzle has made the outside picnic tables useless and I smile when I see the red telephone box at the end of the pub.

Susan looks at me questioningly and I explain how we used to actually stand inside one of these and make phone calls instead of simply grabbing a mobile. Interestingly enough, there is not much of a mobile signal here.

Given that the light will fade in the not-too-distant future, I insist we start our walk. With a rucksack over my shoulder, we head along the winding roads, finding very few people at all. Halfway along the road, a man stops with a tractor asking us where we are going. I tell him we plan to see Gometra and possibly get back and he says we haven't got a hope and asks us to jump on board. He is strong, broad, and jovial with it, so I agree, although to be honest, I think he has more of an eye on Susan than he does on myself.

There is a small bridge we cross that separates Ulva and Gometra and I don't tell him exactly where we are heading but ask, about half a mile after we cross that bridge, that he simply let us go because I have seen some outstanding beauty I want to photograph. He says, 'fair enough' and wishes us all the best and I start to head more overland, cutting away from the road to keep up the pretence that we are here to photograph. Susan has a large camera around her neck and over the last month, I have trained her to use it well.

The site where Keir Matheson was found must have been so remote and I can imagine the hell it must have been for police to investigate this. I wonder if my old friend, Macleod, was on the case. I contacted him before about other things and helped him so I might be able to get some details but rather than sully myself with their investigation, I want to see the place for myself first.

The murder site itself is less than five hundred metres from the sea and I can see a small cove where you can put a landing craft. I gather, in fairness, it is not an easy landing. The crime scene has next to nothing on it. Susan snaps away with her camera and then heads over towards the rocks when I point out the route I would like her to photograph.

We are only about one thousand yards from the road as well, so he could have been dumped from the road. Although

CHAPTER TWO

I am not sure how many cars would travel about here and surely, a car would be noted and spotted. Would your vessel be spotted from the sea if you switched off your identification system—that is, if it even gets picked up here. I wonder if anyone would see you but surely there must be vessels passing by. People forget how busy this part of the world can be with fishermen, dropping their creels here and there . . . there must be fish farms around as well. They see it looks calm, much slower than the motorways we travel along, but in reality, there is plenty that happens.

As I stand staring around me, I can see a small child. I say, small, but she must be around about ten. She is dressed in a raincoat and happily wanders over to me in a fashion mainland kids never would. She has got a bobble hat on that seems to be soaked through but there is a smile on her face.

'Are you staying here?' she asks. 'People don't stay here unless it's the summer, espccially when the weather is like this. Dad says I should say hello to anyone, so hello. What's your name?'

'My name is Paddy,' I say, and what's your name?'

'I'm Jennifer,' she says, and she steps forward holding out her hand. I shake it and tell her it is nice to meet her.

'Why are you here?' she says. 'This is where they found that man.'

'What man?' I say, feigning ignorance.

'The man that was dead,' she said. 'He had no clothes on; no wonder he died out here with no clothes on. You have to wear a jacket, like I do. This keeps me warm,' she says. 'You have a nice jacket on, too. Is that your girlfriend over there?'

I shake my head, 'No, that's not my girlfriend.'

'Is she your wife then?'

Again, I shake my head.

'Your daughter?'

Once more, I shake my head.

'Then why are you out here with her?' asks the little girl.

It is quite an insightful question, one I have to think about how best to answer but then I think, *She's just a kid,* so give an answer that is simple. 'She is just my friend,' I say. Then I call Susan over, as she may be better dealing with kids than I am.

'Hello,' says Susan. 'I'm Susan, and you have met Paddy. What are you doing out here?'

The girl smiles, 'I live over there, it is about . . . oh, Dad says, half a mile. And Dad looks after a lot of sheep here; he keeps an eye on the place. Your friend says you are going to stay tonight.'

'I never said that,' said Paddy. 'I said we might. But like you said, the rain is bad.'

'I wouldn't camp here,' says the girl. 'I have come out here at night before but had to go home.'

'Your dad lets you come out here at night?' says Susan.

'Oh, yes!' she says. 'There is nobody here usually, but I have started to see some things.'

'What do you mean?' asks Susan. 'What things?'

'You hear it, first,' she says. 'It kind of howls. It howls and then it creeps up on you—you hear the thudding of it. Sometimes it roars and I have to run. I have seen it as well. Its eyes are red. They're red and they stare at you.'

'Are there a lot of beasts around here?' I ask. The child shakes her head. 'It's just the one,' she says, 'and it's not here all the time. Maybe you will be lucky; maybe it won't be here tonight and chase you away.'

'When was the last time you saw it?' says Susan.

CHAPTER TWO

'It's been a while,' says the girl, 'and the last time I didn't see it. I heard it but it will come back, I know that. My dad doesn't believe me, but I told him because it was coming for the last six months. It stays all night too sometimes. I know because I came back early one morning and it was still there. It still shouted at me. My dad doesn't believe in the beast, but I do. Do you believe in monsters?'

Susan smiles, 'I think we all have our monsters and demons, don't we? I know Paddy does.'

She gives me a cheeky grin, one that I am struggling with, but in my head, I am just thinking of what the girl is saying. There is nothing here. Looking around, I can see no markings of a beast so all I can think of is that somebody didn't want her about, somebody kind enough not to just get rid of her or maybe he understands that she is from here and her presence will surely be missed. Maybe they don't come often enough. I think I will need to come back here and spend some better time, but the light is fading, and I can see nothing so far. I don't want to waste the hours looking at a site that has nothing.

If the people don't come back very often, this beast doesn't appear, then maybe it's better to come when I know they will be here. I hold my hand out to Jennifer and say thank you, handing her some chocolate. She takes it, greedily stuffing it in her mouth, and then walks over and shakes hands with Susan.

Susan is crouching, bending down to be at the girl's height. I see how comfortable she is, talking to her. The girl goes to turn away, but she suddenly stops and looks at me and says with an innocence of childhood, 'Why do you have no arm?'

I think about telling her how it was blown off, about the explosion that killed several friends, about the months of trauma and trying to put my life back together, about the grief that came with losing a limb, the grief that still comes for me . . . one of the demons and monsters that Susan was speaking of. But I don't. I just say it in three words. 'I lost it.'

The girl nods as if it's a normal thing, turns around and runs off.

'Nicely handled, Paddy,' says Susan. 'She is too young to know any more.'

I agree and tell Susan we need to start heading back because there is nothing around—the ground, everything, there is just nothing but I'm glad I came. I like to visualize things. One of the hard bits in any investigation is being able to see things myself. Now I can.

'Where to, Paddy, then?'

'It is time to grab the ferry before darkness falls,' I say 'and then we head up to the hotel and sit down and eat something. Then we get a good night's sleep because in the morning we are off to see our photographer.'

Susan smiles, takes off her hat, and stuffs it in her pocket. The red hair hangs out the back, blowing in the wind. 'I can nearly go for a swim here,' she says. I look around; the water looks cold and I know it will be worse than it looks. The drizzle is coming down heavier now, almost turning to rain. My cheeks feel like somebody started to put ice cubes on them. Sometimes, I wonder why I took her on and I simply shake my head at her comment.

'You don't know how to live, Paddy,' she says, and marches off. Her hair blows behind her and I recognize in the figure some of the swagger her mother holds. And that is what I need to do tonight, give her a ring. It is not often I hate being away on a case but then again, it has been a long time since I have had anyone to be away from.

Chapter Three

As I look out the window, it's dark, the dawn not yet having decided to interrupt the night. I grab hold of my rain jacket, put it on over my single arm and take a walk out of the hotel. The hotel is one of those made out of former houses and not built for purpose so the route to the front door is across different staircases, flitting here and there between rooms that hide around tight corners. I decide to leave Susan to her sleep and as I stand by the front door, I feel the light wind throwing the drizzle in my face. It's cold and it makes my skin come alive, the hairs indicating every drop that lands on my hand.

Walking through Dervaig does not take long as it is the sort of village that you could drive through without noticing. On the bright side, the road is tight with all the houses close to it and I reckon most people could see what is going on in this village without a second thought. But it is one of those you don't want to speed in as some of the corners you come up to involve you throwing the car around a tight one and if anyone was coming the other way, the chances of you smacking into them is very likely.

I stretch my legs for about an hour and rather than trying for the circuitous route of which I am unsure, I simply walk out for about half an hour and then walk back. By the time I reach the hotel, the sun starts to climb, cracks in the daylight begin to emerge, and I see a figure that I recognize standing on the road.

She has a camera around her neck and is dressed in a smart leather jacket. It is three-quarter length and compliments her black jeans. The jacket being slightly open, I can see the crisp blue t-shirt underneath, and I wonder how she does not just feel frozen standing there. As I get closer, there is a smile and the hands ruffle the hair and she gives me that cheeky look that her mother also has.

Damn it, that's what I didn't do—I didn't ring Maggie. I make a mental note to do that before turning to her daughter and asking if she slept well.

'Morning, Paddy, you're up early. Why didn't you give me a knock? I would have come out for the walk with you.'

'I'm not used to having a partner,' I say, 'and anyway, I thought you could do with a rest. That was quite a hike we did yesterday.'

Most people would probably think Susan is the fitter of the two of us but she is still only in her teens and when you have to trudge along for miles, you find out that a lot of them run out of steam as the day progresses. I'm not quick but I can walk all day. I looked down at her camera. 'So, you are all ready to go then?' I say. 'I thought we might have some breakfast first.'

She laughs. 'I didn't know where you were or if you were on the go already,' she said. 'Come on then, let's eat.'

For someone with such a slim figure, Susan certainly knows how to eat. Don't get me wrong—she's not wiry, instead being quite full in her figure; it's just that it's trim, a trait her mother probably had in her day but now she is growing that little bit of middle-age spread that we all have. Not that I don't love her for it. Susan is packing away sausages and bacon, as well as the beans and anything else that's on the plate whereas I'm sat eating my cereal. Maybe it's because I have a woman in my life that I'm starting to try and look after my figure because before I didn't. Or maybe, I'm scared her daughter will report about how bad my eating habits are. If that's the case, I need to knock that on the head quickly.

'So, you want to go and see the man he was staying with today?' asks Susan.

'Yes,' I say, 'I think we should pay him a visit now that I have seen the lie of the land. I didn't want to go before I understood Gometra and how it looked just in case he refers to any of it. He is down by Calgary Bay, which if you remember we passed by yesterday in the car, although it was dark. I've sailed round there before but never been on the actual bay itself. From the maps on the phone, it looks like his house is quite secluded just off the road, but it has a view of the bay with several things beside it. Oh, and Susan, by the way, you look the part. I especially like the jacket.'

'Really?' she says smiling. 'It's Mum's. She's had it for years but told me to wear it. She said it's starting to get a bit tight so maybe you should buy her a new one, Paddy.'

'Right, then,' I said. 'Here are some rules, out here on work, that's all off limits. I don't need your advice on how to look after your mother; what your mother and I do is also off limits, understood?'

I gave her a strong eye as if I were being completely serious and she retreats back for a moment before understanding what I'm doing. 'I get you, Paddy,' she says laughing, 'You had me there.'

'Come on, finish up,' I say. 'Let's get down the road here and see our man.'

The road to Calgary Bay continues in the short, winding style that we are used to on the island and now that the daylight's out, there is a bit more traffic on the move. I almost miss the house surrounded by trees, but Susan grabs my shoulder and indicates with her finger the oncoming secluded entrance. Spinning the car round, I take it up the short drive and park in front of what is a rather large home, having at least three stories I can see, and a front porch that looks enormous.

In the drive, I see a Porsche along with a smart BMW and I wonder if this guy is really a photographer. The drizzle is continuing as we step out of the car and as our feet crunch across the gravel path, I can see someone looking out of a window above. It's a female face, older, and when I press the doorbell, she disappears back inside.

A young woman answers the door dressed in one of those house-cleaning coats, quite old style, and one that looks completely out of place as she can only be about twenty.

'Hello there, my name is Patrick Smythe; can I talk to Mr Doolan, please?'

'Okay, I think he's here,' says the woman. 'I'll just go and get Jack for you; can you just wait there?'

We stand in the drizzle for a good three minutes before there is a shuffling of feet in the distance and a short man comes to the door. His hair is fighting a losing battle and what remains is cropped and cut close to his skin. It's retaining its dark, natural colour and I wonder if that's a cover up from some of those wonderful chemicals people put on their hair or if he is actually just one of the fortunate few. I haven't been affected by hair loss yet, but having seen my father and grandfather, it's on its

CHAPTER THREE

way. The man is dressed in a gown that goes all the way to a pair of slippers on his feet and he seems quite perturbed to have visitors at this time of the day.

'Kyla said your name is Smythe; is that correct?'

'Yes sir, my name is Patrick Smythe. I am here on behalf of Mrs Matheson. I believe her son was here with you for a time before he was unfortunately found dead on Gometra. I am looking into it at her request so I was wondering if I could have a small amount of your time to fill in some blanks that she was unable to do for me.'

'So, you are a private investigator, is that correct?' The man looks at me, his eyes narrowing as if I am the scum of the earth. 'And who is this with you?' he says, his eyes turning to Susan, widening, a thin smile coming across his face. I see him look down, noting her camera. His eyes continue and I see he is looking at the rest of her figure.

'That's correct. This is my associate, Susan Caulderwood; she will be joining us if that's okay.'

'That will be absolutely fine,' says the man and I think that Susan might have been my ticket in today.

The man steps aside and asks us to go through, letting me go ahead and then joining beside Susan. He takes us through to a large conservatory at the rear of the house before shouting for Kyla, his domestic, to bring us some tea. He starts off giving me some general chit-chat about the island and I ask him how long he has been in photography.

'I got my first camera when I was six,' he says, 'and ever since then, I have taken photographs, but it was only when I was twenty-three that I managed to make a living from it. I have spent my life doing weddings, portraits, family gatherings, and it is only recently that I have been able to get awards for nature.

I am not messing about, Mr Smythe; it's a good living and it's what I am able to do because of my wife.'

'I believe I may have seen her at the window, earlier on,' I say. 'What does your wife do?'

'She is a doctor,' he says, 'a consultant actually; she travels away to London quite often, and this is our second home but it's where I spend most of my time. She flits back and forward on various committees doing certain research. I really don't understand everything she does, and I don't need to. I am quite happy when she is away, walking round this island and taking my photographs. I have a studio in the back room where I can develop them as well because I still use the old techniques sometimes, as well as the modern ones. That's the trouble with a lot of the modern-day photographers who cannot develop their own. What about you, love, are you able to develop your own?'

Susan smiles and shakes her head. 'I'm only really getting into photography,' she says. 'I did a course and that, but the course doesn't teach you everything, does it? But at the moment, I'm just doing photographs for Paddy. You don't need to have such an artistic eye with those.' Susan smiles and I can see what she is doing, reeling him in for comment. I am not sure he is that gullible though he is enjoying the smile.

'So, what can you tell me about Keir Matheson?' I say. 'Was he up here long?'

'No, Mr Smythe, he actually wrote to me, asking me if he could join me for a while and given some of the work that the young man did, I decided it would be good for him, and possibly for me, if he came up. We had plenty of room in the house, the wife being away a lot, so I felt a friend who enjoyed a similar pursuit to myself would be a good thing.

CHAPTER THREE

'He was up here for about three months and I got him away doing night shoots as well as the normal day-time things. Photography at night can be a lot more exciting, a lot riskier. He would go down to the coast and he'd gotten to a stage where I wanted him to go himself and see what he could do.

'The night it happened I knew he'd gone out, but I had no idea where and when he didn't come back the next morning, I called the police. They found him on Gometra, naked and without his camera gear. I was shocked but I had absolutely no idea what happened to him.'

'Did he leave anything at the house?' I ask.

'He did but the police have everything; they took away all of my gear as well as that he was using, quite a significant piece of kit, to extract all of the files. But hopefully they will be returning it, though as it is an open case at the moment, that could be a while. I have heard from friends it can take over a year.'

'Well, I'm sure they will be as quick as they can,' I say. 'So, was he going to Gometra that night that he went out?'

'I don't believe he was,' says Mr Doolan. 'Because when I saw him leave, he didn't have substantial gear with him and he crossed straight over to the bay opposite the house. I thought he was only going out for a couple of hours. There's plenty around the bay you can shoot at night. I was used to going to bed and have him coming in much later as I believe he had also picked up some younger friends. I didn't know them that well. I'm sure he must have had some larks with them, maybe popping down to some of our local pubs. I don't frequent them myself; I am happier here with a glass of my own wine but maybe they could give you some details.

'I don't really know that much about the kid because we

didn't talk about much else other than photography. I can tell you that he was a good photographer prepared to go and look for a photograph. Who knows what sort of trouble he got into that he ended up like that? You can pass on my condolences to his mother. I sent the card and that, but I've never met her.'

There is a clatter and a tall woman enters the room. She is in the latter stages of her life I reckon, sixty-plus, but she is tall and elegant and gives off a picture of class despite the fact that she is wearing jeans and a t-shirt.

'This is my wife, the great doctor,' says Doolan without a hint of sarcasm. 'Annie, this is Mr Smythe and his associate, Susan.'

I notice that Annie looks at Susan with daggers and I guess she is used to Jack talking to other women. 'They are here to look into Keir's disappearance,' he says, and the woman's face suddenly becomes sombre.

'I wish you all the best with that, Mr Smythe, because he was a nice kid. I wasn't here in those last weeks. I was down in London, working, so I am afraid I have little to help you with; all I can say is it's a great shame because he showed Jack's promise with a camera. I have to go out now so I'm sorry and accept my apologies for not being able to speak longer. Don't be long, Jack—you know you've got plenty to do,' she says, and I see her eyes flick to Susan and back to Jack.

After she leaves, I decide there is not much else to learn at this time. 'You say they took all the equipment; did they clear his entire room?'

'That's correct,' says Mr Doolan, 'so there is nothing even there to show you; you'd be looking at what is effectively a changed room.'

'Well, thank you for that then, sir; I will get out of your way,' and I think to myself that I need to get hold of some of the police

CHAPTER THREE

contacts and see what gear Keir had and what photographs are in there.

I wonder what Macleod is up to at the moment.

Once again, I am ushered ahead, and Jack seems to accompany Susan to the front door. As I turn around to thank him, I notice he is standing with his arm behind her and it moves up, reaching into her neck where he starts to rub. That seems a little forward to me and I can see in her face she is not comfortable with it, but I say my goodbyes and together we sit in the car.

'Was that dirty bugger rubbing your neck on you?' I ask.

'Yes,' she said, 'I thought I should just go with it, didn't want to show any antagonism in case we need him again.'

'There's a time and a place to play somebody,' I say to Susan, 'but all we have done is ask questions and he is already trying to feel you up, so you need to put a foot on that. Anyone does that again, just turn round and knock their hand off and tell them you're not that sort of girl.'

'Okay,' she says, 'I will do—thanks, Paddy.'

'And if I ever want you to play along, I will tell you specifically,' I say, 'because you have to be in agreement for that and it's not something you do lightly. But now I need to get hold of the police and find out where Keir's gear's gone—see if I can get a hold of it.'

'Do you want me to come along for that?' says Susan.

'No,' I say, 'your job is to find out what his wife does, who she is, and how she does it and find out how much she is about here and then, if you get a chance, get round the local pubs wherever they are, see if our Keir did like a drink. Because at the moment, we haven't got a lot; Susan, I am afraid there is a lot more digging to be done before the day is out.'

Chapter Four

One of the key things about being an investigator is to build up relationships with the police force of the state you're in. I've been fortunate in that some investigations have led me to discover illegal activities that I'm then able to hand over to said police, who then make an arrest and feel particularly happy about my involvement. This is not always the case but when it is, you tend to make a friend, a professional friend, whom you can call on for other favours. Given that Keir appeared to be murdered, I believe that certain detectives would have been involved; there are a large number of detectives working murder cases so I may not get lucky, but I usually can get some influence. Plus, my contact's a Detective Inspector and has a large number of years within the force.

In the not-so-recent past, I managed to hand him significant leads in finding killers of his own. I also broke into a major human trafficking ring for which he took a lot of credit. Now, don't think of it that way; he wasn't stealing my thunder because I wanted to stay in the dark. Sometimes, I shouldn't bring my connections to light. But he was grateful, I have his number and it's the one I'm going to use now.

'Macleod,' says the voice on the other end of the line. It's got a hint of Glasgow in it, more something imported, rather than bread and butter Glasgow because he carries one of those accents that people from outside of Scotland don't identify as Scottish. One of the joys of Scotland is that it has so many accents, but the outside world always thinks of the Glaswegian one as being definitive Scottish. Back home, because of our Ulster Scots roots, we can sometimes do that as well but it would be like someone coming to the province not understanding about the Ballymena accent, the Belfast accent, or indeed, the quieter, more subtle Armagh accent—all part of the same place, the same language.

'Hello, Detective Inspector, it's your favourite one-armed man. How are you doing today?'

'Mr Smythe,' says the voice, and I'm not sure he's entirely pleased to hear me. 'Is this a social call looking for my health and well-being or is there something I can do for you? Or even better, is there something you can do for me?'

'I'm afraid, Inspector, that this time, I'm calling in a favour and I do believe that you owe me one so if you don't mind, I'll get to it. Are you busy today?'

'Currently in the office in Inverness; why do you ask?' he says, his tone is becoming more clipped so maybe he does have work on. 'So, what is it you're after?' asks Macleod.

'I don't know if you've heard of the body found on Gometra near the Isle of Mull. Young lad called Keir Matheson found stark bollock naked on the island, no equipment. Apparently, you guys ran the case and took all his gear away from the place he was staying at. He was a photographer and I need to get a look at his equipment for the photographs he was taking.'

'What's your interest in it, Paddy?' says Macleod, his tone serious but not unfriendly.

'The mother approached me and asked me to look into it,

thought you guys weren't getting anywhere. I'm not sure there's anywhere to get either but at the moment, it's hard digging up things. I'm on Mull, just going through all the usual processes, the people he lived with, the people he met but I could do with looking at what items or equipment he had with him here because he didn't send any of them down to his mother. Were you on the case, Macleod?'

'No,' he says, 'and neither was McGrath; it wasn't Ross either. It was one of the other sections. So, what is it you need?'

'Specifically, can you get me images that he had on his computers; that he had on his cameras. You should have lifted them all off by now, any other photographs of the case and if you've got any ideas where to start, that would be helpful as well.'

'Are you on Mull at the moment?' asks Macleod, 'Because you know that the desk stuff can't go anywhere. You have to come and see it.'

'I can be with you in maybe two to three hours?'

'No,' says Macleod, 'I know you and I know what you want. Don't come near the station.' He gives me an address that's just north of Inverness. 'Go there,' he says. 'There'll be a woman expecting you. Be polite to her and I'll join you there but don't arrive until seven o'clock tonight.'

Having been given my instructions, I get hold of Susan and meet her for lunch. It's about two o'clock when I leave her to catch the ferry and start driving towards Inverness. Going over on foot, I hire a car in Oban. I've got a few things I can do, and I stop off at a contact, Martha, the woman who hacks into computer systems for me and finds things out about people. I'm getting her to do a background check on Jack Doolan to see if everything's legit and also on his wife. None of them

CHAPTER FOUR

appear to be anything other than they say they are, but it's always worth having a look to check, especially when it comes to money. Money doesn't show on people's faces—it shows in their bank accounts. Martha's good at getting it.

When I get to Inverness, I do a couple of errands, including picking up a rather stylish black, three-quarter-length leather coat. As if reminded by the purchase, I call Maggie and we chat for an hour. We're still in the early days of seeing each other so we have still got plenty to talk about. I've had to leave *Craigantlet* for a week but she's sailing my boat around the West Coast. She's currently going past Ardnamurchan Point and enjoying herself. It's just my luck to pick up a sailor and I reckon our little boat is going to enjoy the company of a woman on board as well.

I'm pretty buoyed by the time I've finished the phone call and I find myself somewhere for a bite to eat before taking a walk. Killing time before meeting someone is always the worst but I manage to make it pass before heading north of Inverness, taking a road off at Kessock, driving through various tree-lined roads before coming down to the edge of the firth where the view takes my breath away. I look left to see the firth stretching out to sea, the vastness impressing upon me. Whereas if I look right, I see the bridge that links this island across to Inverness, a monument to man's engineering. But what really grabs me are those endless ripples across the firth and I can feel myself missing my boat. Yet what I don't know, is it *Craigantlet* I'm missing or is it Maggie? Maybe it's both.

I get out of the car and walk up to a pleasant house, its gardens looking tidy. It's secluded away from prying eyes and as I rap on the front door, I hear a jovial woman shout, 'I'm coming!' The door swings open and she's standing in a skirt and t-shirt with a full figure and a smiling face.

'It's you, you came here before,' she said. 'You were looking for Seoras last time.' Seoras is Macleod's first name but I don't call him by that. I guess that's for people he really likes.

'Yes, and you must be Jane. The last time I didn't say I knew your name.' I can see her staring at where my left arm should be and then she feels self-conscious about it, looking up into my face, and I'm waiting for the apology.

'I'm sorry. I just—uh—I don't see many people with a missing arm. It's very rude of me; please come in. Seoras said we were expecting you. Straight through, out to the terrace at the back,' she says. 'I'm afraid he's going to be running about half an hour late. Do you drink?'

I don't actually drink even when I have the need to be social, so I shake my hand and ask if she's got any tea. She waves me on out to the terrace. It has one of those stylish wooden benches that you can swing your legs round and then underneath so that two people will be facing each other rather close. It's one of those glorified picnicking sight benches except this one's made of quality wood and doesn't look like it's going to fall apart anytime soon. A pot of tea arrives in a china mug and I gratefully take it, supping it down because I am feeling somewhat parched. Traveling does that to you, catches you out because you don't feel like you're exerting a lot of force. You don't feel tired but all the time you're dehydrating slowly.

It's a pleasant half hour I spend in the company of Macleod's partner, Jane, and she certainly has a pleasant demeanour to match the view in front of me. I can see why he likes her. She's quite a contrast to his drab style, a woman who's able to poke fun to the correct level depending who she's talking to. Eventually, Macleod comes onto the patio and nods at me

CHAPTER FOUR

before embracing his wife.

'If you boys are talking shop, I shall get out of the way,' says Jane and I stand up reaching across to shake her hand.

'It's been an absolute delight,' I say. 'I hope it's not the last time we meet.' She looks quite charmed, smiles at me, and tells me I'm welcome anytime. When I sit back down, Macleod's opposite and staring at me.

'When she says, 'Welcome, anytime',' he says, 'she's just being polite. If you want to come here, you phone me first.'

I think about a joke but to be honest, he doesn't look in the joking mood. Macleod always seems to have a certain standard that you don't cross and considering I need stuff from him, I'm not in the mood to cross them. So, I simply mention what a delightful woman she is and let's get down to business.

Macleod pulls out a folder containing various pictures. 'This is a large section of the file; you can sit and open it up here and have a look. Take notes if you want but whatever happens to them, I never saw them, nobody else ever saw them and you destroy them when you're done with them, is that understood?'

I don't even bother to look up, just say yes as if this is the most ridiculous comment he's made because I know all of this and get down to looking through what's in front of me. Most of it shows the investigation struggled to get off the ground. They went door to door but found extraordinarily little. The background of the boy shows nothing. Why he's dead seems to be a complete mystery. There are a lot of photographs of places he'd taken, which I identify and indeed are all round that area of Mull but there's nothing seemingly untoward in it. Certainly not something I can see at the pace I'm going at.

'Of course, if something was going on there, his death might have put a stop to that,' said Macleod, 'or they might just have lain low for a while. You might be there at the right time, Mr Smythe.'

'Paddy, please, just call me Paddy. Mr Smythe sounds too formal.'

'And Seoras is out of the question. It's Macleod or Detective Inspector. I think I know you well enough that you can use Macleod.'

'You are not that happy doing this, are you, bringing the records out?'

'No, I am not,' he says, 'but you've done me good turns and you've kept your word so none of this goes out of your hands or gets lost and it all gets destroyed when you're done and you were never here—I think we understand that, don't we?'

I wave my hand up in the air again acknowledging that this is ridiculous that he needs to tell me but then he puts something in front of me. It's one of those USB sticks that you plug into the front of a computer.

'What's that?' I ask.

'It's every picture from his camera, from his computer, the lot—and that one, I want back. You make no copies off that stick; you only view off the stick and the stick comes back to me.'

'I understand,' I say, 'anything of use on it?'

'If there was,' he says, 'I'm sure the boys in Glasgow would still be investigating. I'm afraid you might find a dead-end, Mr Smythe, but then again, you might have a bit more about you than that so I wish you all the best and kindly ask you to get out of my house and remember the address. It's an address you never give anyone.'

I stand up, pocket the USB stick, and reach across with my hand. Macleod shakes it firmly and holds my stare.

CHAPTER FOUR

'I don't mind talking about cases, especially if I've been on them but don't make it a habit to ask me to take evidence out and share it with you that's locked in somebody else's case and they don't know you've got it—they don't know I've got it and it's not something I like to do. So, by all means, I'll discuss something with you but don't ask me again to pull evidence out like this, especially at the start of something. You could at least have waited until you reckoned he was murdered properly, and you needed to catch the culprits.'

I raise my hand up to my forehead and give the American salute partly to show the recognition of what he's done and partly because I think he's being a prat giving me this hard line. I've been nothing but professional so it must be bothering him having to do this.

The drive back in the dark to Mull isn't the most enjoyable but I use my mobile to contact Maggie again. When the signal dies out, I try the radio. I fight to stay awake. At Oban I catch a lift on a fishing vessel, sailing up the Sound of Mull which drops me at Craignure and back to my car.

On arriving back at Dervaig, I see the light on in Susan's room and I make my way quickly up to her. When she opens the door, she's standing in a pair of pyjamas. I try to look the other way.

'I've got photographs for us to look at,' I say. 'Put something on and come next door.' Five minutes later, she is sat wrapped up in a dressing gown kneeling on the floor beside me as we look through my laptop at the photographs Macleod's given me.

As we go through each one, we spot where they are and see plenty of pictures of Ulva, Gometra, Calgary Bay but a few of the others I don't recognize and in honesty, it's not easy because nobody's tagged them and that's unusual. Most photographers I know who are any good like to record a photograph: where it is, how they took it. Some of the others certainly have the detail in the metadata of the file but there's a couple of beaches where the metadata is missing. The file name gives no clue either and it makes me wonder what those beaches are.

'I think we have found your work for the next couple of days,' I tell Susan. 'I think you need to go to beaches—find out where these are.'

'What are you going to do?' she says.

'I'm going to leave you for a couple of days,' I tell her, 'and take a little camping trip to Gometra. I just need to see if Keir's body scared people off for good.'

Chapter Five

Having left Susan to her own devices and reiterating to her not to get into trouble, I take the car and drive down to Ulva to catch the ferry across to Gometra. The forecast isn't looking good, and as I arrive, I see the grey clouds swinging past the backdrop of the islands, the rain clearly visible on the water. The small ferry trip across is pleasant. It's short, and I find myself somewhat more relaxed than the normal. This is me back to being myself, out on my own, just putting my nose in places.

I've left the car at the Ulva-ferry side and I have a pack on my back containing a tent, some supplies that I had to pop to Tobermory to buy, and, of course, my camera. Once I cross over, I have a bite to eat in a little pub that sits on Ulva. It's a popular spot in the summer and even now you get a couple of people making their way across but there's not many others who decide to take a walk any further.

Unlike last time, I don't follow the road but cut across country, trying to keep out of people's noses. I pitch my tent up on Gometra but a little distance away from where we met Jennifer before. That's where I'm going to watch but I don't want to do it in such an obvious fashion that nobody will come near the place. Jennifer said there was a monster, something with red eyes that came. In truth, she didn't strike me as an over-imaginative child, but I guess I'll find out over the next couple of days.

The morning rolls into the afternoon when I pitch my tent, cook myself some beans, and then take a walk down to the shores. The water looks cold, not that it isn't always, up here in Scotland. If you jumped in there and stayed in for like twenty minutes, you'd probably freeze, arms heaving up, start to sink down. That's if the current didn't pull you down anyway. I take a look at my mobile phone and see I'm struggling for a signal; however, I did manage to download a few messages before I came across on the island and I have some reports to examine.

The various accounts that have been sent through to me don't seem to show up much and it's been a fruitless afternoon poring through them on the mobile phone. I've got a backup battery in here, but I need to be careful with it or I'll run out of charge in no time and that'll leave me without any music through the night. That's a rather depressing thought and as the rain comes in and starts to pour down, I begin to wonder if these few nights of camping were a bad idea.

At about three a.m., I take a walk around the site we were at before where Jennifer said she saw the beast. The night's wet and windy and I struggle to see much further than twenty feet ahead due to the darkness. I have a pocket light, but I choose not to use it in case anyone's looking around thinking that someone's here. If people are coming ashore and doing anything, or indeed operating in any other capacity, the last thing I want them to do is see me or my light flickering about, scaring them off.

It's about seven o'clock when I get back to the tent, having seen nothing all night, and I sleep through the morning. By

CHAPTER FIVE

lunchtime, I'm back up, having cooked myself some sausages. I make my way over again to see Jennifer walking around and decide I won't bother her in case she makes a thing of why I'm back again. When she disappears, I take a few more photographs of the area, but nothing seems to have changed. This search is seeming pretty fruitless at this point in time.

I rest up through the evening, falling asleep again to wake up at one in the morning. In truth, I'm pretty cold, beginning to smell and could do with a proper wash. Tomorrow, I might even pop down to the sea and wash myself in it or find some sort of small river. Or maybe I'll take a walk back and eat something at a little pub, grab a wash in their sinks.

Once again, I don my jacket and head out into driving rain and I can feel the numbness in my legs and the chill across my knees—it's an effort to keep driving forward. I do have a good pair of boots though; my feet are dry but everything else feels like it's beginning to get soaked. I'm not daft; I have waterproofs on, but they seem to be able to take only so much and not any more, or maybe it's just the sweat inside that makes me feel damp.

This time as I head towards the burial ground, I look out to sea. There are a few boats about; most are far off in the distance but there's one displaying its light, the light that all boats have to display at night just so they don't bump into each other. I settle down in the grass, taking what shelter I can behind a lump in the terrain and then pop my head back up to see if the boat's still there. To my surprise, the light's gone out. I wait, checking again along the line of sight I had before but the light's still not there. Now maybe it's just a faulty light or maybe they've switched it off for some good reason, but I'm an investigator so I don't look for the good reasons—I look for the bad ones.

Standing up and then scrambling across to where the rocks drop to the shore, I hunker down again, staring into the driving rain. I hear the lap of the sea, the waves as they crash against the rocks, but I hear something else on the wind. Is that someone talking? Are those voices? It's hard to distinguish in the night when the wind races back and forward, hard to know when your hood's wrapped around your head so tight just to keep out the rain and the cold.

I hold my position, just waiting, knowing that I'm not that far away from the only path I found up from the rocks the previous time we visited. My patience is rewarded an hour and a half later. There's a small dinghy, which cuts through the waves and manages to pull in alongside at the small piece of shore. They must have got buffeted quite hard coming in and it's certainly not a journey I would make out of any sort of pleasure. Granted, it's also the middle of the morning, I know nobody who would be out in this weather without some sort of nefarious purpose.

I don a pair of infrared glasses from my backpack and as I stare out, I can pick up two figures making their way up. Now, well clear of the shoreline I'm walking across. They also have lights on them and I have to take the goggles off to realise the lights are red, held in front of them, apart at a distance that may well look to a child like some sort of monster's eyes.

Pulling my goggles back on, I see that they both carry backpacks. It's hard to gage what a person looks like through infrared goggles. In terms of height, they're both around about 5'10 and they seem young in the way that they move, the light step, nothing to show any signs of age at all so they could be anything from their teens to about their thirties. A couple of spades appear and they start digging the ground carefully, lifting up turf, finding cracks that have been there before. Once the ground has been moved to one side, they drop something in, packets from their backpacks before working the ground back down again and carefully replacing the grass and heather over the top. Once completed, they quickly make their way back. I see them descend down the rocks and then head off in the boat.

This is certainly behaviour that's worthy of my attention and part of me thinks I should go out there, dig up, and find what's there already but I'd rather do it with a bit of daylight so I can put everything back correctly. They used little light so it can't be that difficult. I also don't want to go near the site, because if I dig it up, I'll have to use my torch and if the boat is still out there, they could see someone working away and come back or even just stop using the place so with a weariness, I trudge back to my tent, open it up, strip off my wet clothing, and climb inside my sleeping bag.

The morning's beginning to come and I fall asleep around about five o'clock, waking up with the sunlight coming through by ten. The clouds have broken somewhat and they're beginning to stop for a while and a part of me wants to head back to that nice pub, warm up, get some good food, and get a wash but I need to be quick, check over what's happening.

Walking back out, I find Jennifer playing around the spot, and this time I can't avoid her. She's bound to recognise the one-armed man.

'Hello, mister,' she says, 'you must really like it here?'

I nod my head, 'I do, Jennifer, just like yourself. What are you doing playing out here? Haven't you got some sort of school to go to?'

'Not today,' she says. 'I normally have to go to the ferry but not today.' That's all I get, no explanation beyond that and I don't push, instead walking over and sitting down looking out to the sea; there's no boat there now—there's certainly nothing that seems to be carrying anyone nefarious.

I see a creel boat go past as I wait for Jennifer to disappear. She takes two hours and I end up pulling out my little stove and making myself some tea while I'm waiting. I'm chilled, having never really gotten past the cold from last night and as the rain starts to come in again, I watch her head for home.

Walking over to the patch of ground from last night, it takes a while for my eyes to adjust and I fall to my knees, hands tracing around the grass. I find a small indent cleverly hidden because they don't cut through what heather lies on top. It's old and if you put a spade through it straight away, you would cut it and make a channel. They have managed to lift it back up and then cut down and around.

As I do it, I'm able to peel back the grass quite easily to reveal a square of only about two foot. Using a small spade of my own, I'm able to dig away the dirt and go down a couple of feet to what's a very, very shallow hiding hole. There's a tin down there and as I open the lid, I see the packets inside. They are white, probably drugs.

Carefully, I take one out. It's completely sealed and I wonder how I'm going to get some of the gear out without showing that the bags were cut into. I check through them all until I find one that's been taped back down. It's obviously the one that somebody's checked. Carefully, I peel back the sticky tape, I take a small vial from my backpack, dropping some of the powder into it before carefully taping it back down again. I replace everything, putting the soil back, then rolling back the turf.

In fairness, it's very neatly done and if I hadn't seen them do it, I'm not sure I'd have found it. I head off back to my tent and think about packing up. Surely that will be it but what if they come back and move the drugs at some point. Something tells me to wait and so while it's daylight, I make that trip back to the pub at the Ulva ferry, fill myself up with a rather good steak and chips before spending half an hour in their bathroom washing myself down. It might seem like a long time to you, but I've got one arm.

The woman behind the bar asks me how I'm getting on and I tell her it's great, having picked up a lot of good photographs of birds. I can only talk a bit about ornithology but it didn't make me look like I'm a rank amateur, which in truth I am. She says the weather's heading in again and I probably don't want to be out in a tent tonight. I can understand that as the north of Scotland often gets battered, but I think I want to give it one more go. So again, I head back to my tent and fall asleep around about eight o'clock, waking up about one.

The weather at this point is extremely rough but regardless, I continue my way across to the site I was at before and spot another light out at sea. Once again, I spend another couple of hours in the dark before a pair of figures arrive. I watch them go through the same ritual before making their way back down to the boat but this time, I need more information.

I already know what they're doing, but I need to know who's doing it and so I follow them, trailing them back using the rain and the wind as my cover. It's tough going climbing down the rocks because I can't take the path they're using but instead have to head off a little distance, scrambling down a cliff face and then holding my position. I can hear the motor of a boat but this one is small; it'll be the tender going back to the main vessel.

With the weather, my face gets battered and I feel like my nose is about to drop off. I hear that put-put sound, voices pulling people in, someone telling someone else to shut up and be quiet. I then hear a main engine kick in and the boat's starting to pull away. In the dark, I can't see anything, and I wonder how they can, but they'll be operating on a GPS, looking out, following the chart on an electronic screen, no doubt.

As I look out into the distance, I can just about pick up a faint haze of a screen on a man's face. It's too indistinct; I have no way of telling what he looks like or indeed if it's even a man but as they continue to steam, there's a light that comes on and then more lights surround the vessel, just simple basic ones that you would use if you were travelling anywhere in the dark. I put up my binoculars and scan the boat, but all figures are distant, hazy.

I need one thing to tie them down, one thing to know who they are. I could check the Automatic Information System, the AIS, but I doubt they will be using that if they want to be this nefarious. And it's then I catch it. It's at the side of the boat when the clouds roll back and a shaft of moonlight comes through. I'm fortunate; the binoculars are sweeping past at the time, and I managed to clock two words: *Sandra Jane*, it says and as I hang there on the cliff, I feel slightly warmer.

I mull the words in my head, *Sandra Jane*, walking back over towards my tent. Once again, it's around five o'clock when I reach there but I don't go to bed, I simply pack up. It is not easy in that wind but having stuffed everything inside my ruck, I then begin to walk back and catch the first ferry across from

CHAPTER FIVE

Ulva to Mull. By nine o'clock, I'm in my hotel room making my way for a shower which I stand under for half an hour trying to drive away the cold of the previous nights. The *Sandra Jane*? If I can get out, I might even find them before they've landed.

Chapter Six

Susan must have been up and out early because when I got back to the hotel, she wasn't about, her room was locked, and although it's not in any significant way locked, I'm not going to pry just to find out where she is. At the end of the day, I sent her out to do a little bit of digging so hopefully that's where she is and I'll soon catch up with her later.

On my laptop, I search up the vessel *Sandra Jane* and I find a local one. It apparently does pleasure tours. I doubt at this time of the year that much happens, but we could always try it. I'm sure there's plenty of birds around to be spotted, so I give the phone number that's on the website a ring, and I get told it'll be a while before they can get to a decent pier for me. I advise I'm in Dervaig and I suggest that maybe Tobermory would be a good place to meet up. This would take me out of my way, take me down into the Sound and put plenty of distance between where I am and where I was. The voice on the other end says okay, and to meet them over there round about lunchtime. I guess they must have continued round through the night, so I manage to get a couple of hours' sleep before jumping in the car again and driving the short distance to Tobermory.

The place is incredibly picturesque with its coloured build-

CHAPTER SIX

ings along the bay and I wander around for a bit, grabbing some lunch before I'm due to meet them. I'm in that state where I haven't had a lot of sleep, I've been cold, and my body just feels very fragile, but I still remember to pack a bag and look like a bird spotter, or at least some sort of wildlife person. There is a zoom on my camera which with one hand is rather awkward as you have to adjust it then move your hand back to actually take the photographs. It's a bit weird and it's not a great hobby of mine so I'm not looking forward to trying to make this look natural.

I see the boat coming into the harbour as I'm standing beside the Coastguard Station looking at the orange lifeboat. Considering the area, Tobermory is a reasonably busy port and I flag the vessel down seeing a young man waving back to me. I reckon he is about twenty-five and I see another two crew on board.

'Hello there, Mr MacIver,' says the man. That's the alias I gave myself. The trouble with Smythe in this part of the world is that it's pretty easy to remember, especially with a Paddy in front of it.

'Hi,' I say. 'Joe MacIver, delighted to meet you,' pressing my single hand into the man's and shaking it vigorously. 'I'd like to get going as soon as we can,' I say. 'Did you see any wildlife on the way round, any seals or dolphins, anything, maybe spot a couple of birds as well?'

'Well, there's the bits and pieces, we will take you down the Sound today and then back up, if that's all right with you but to be honest, we can only manage a couple of hours.'

I nod, realizing they've been up all night and they're probably feeling as bad as me if not worse. 'What's your name by the way, skipper?' I ask.

'Andrew,' he says, 'delighted to have you on board.' He offers no more and I get the feeling he never was going to, so I push on.

'And who's your two friends?'

'That's Digsy and that's John.' I wonder about the man's accent because it's not from here. Instead it's got a distinctly English twang and I would probably place it on the east coast. As I settle down onboard and they turn the boat back towards the Sound, I hear them talk in low conversation and realize that their accents are from Lincolnshire.

'What you boys doing up here?' I say. 'It's a long way from home.'

'Running a business,' says Andrew; 'you can't get much in the fishing these days even though we were brought up to it.'

I nod my head and shout, 'Grimsby, was it somewhere over that way?' He simply nods his head and I get little else from him as he takes the boat out into the Sound.

The Sound of Mull is a compact piece of water, and we pass Calve Island and head out into the main body separating Mull from the mainland. One of the ferries passes by and I realize just how restrictive this place is after the vast expanses of water I'm used to sailing. I take out my camera and pretend to take some scenic photographs but every now and again, I swing it round and try and catch them, picking up a face. It's not easy, because I can't make it look as if I'm photographing them, just having the camera resting on my lap and trying to judge. It's only after I've taken some other photographs, more scenic pictures, that I can look at the rear of it and go through the shots I've taken to see if I have their faces.

Andrew, the skipper, is six-foot-tall, a broad build of a man with blond hair. He looks like a fisherman, arms that are strong and a grim, chiselled face that should belong to somebody twice his age. Digsy, on the other hand, is only about five foot five and is cheeky with his slightly ginger hair. It's that sort of auburn colour where it's fading out of brown heading towards ginger, but it's failed miserably. Digsy seems to be the runt of the place, running around, bringing drinks to Andrew and basically doing whatever his bidding is. John is only slightly shorter than Andrew and seems quite close to him, but his hair is jet black and he sports a beard which is tightly cropped in the modern style. He comes over to sit beside me and stares at the lack of a left arm.

'How do you manage?' he says, as if it's nothing unusual about what he's asking.

'I'm sorry?' I ask. 'How do I manage what?'

'With the arm, just a single arm.'

'It's something you get used to,' I say, 'a bit like the sea; it's a bit rough, isn't it?'

The man laughs, 'You could say that. Are you able to hold the camera steady enough? Any chance I could look at some of the photographs?'

I have to think on my feet, 'I've just filled the card,' I said, 'I'm just changing into another one, just give me a moment and then I'll show you.' I dig inside the bag, pull out another memory card, taking the other one out and slipping this one in. The previous one is nowhere near full but it gives me a good excuse. After I've completed the operation, I stand and take some photographs of the scenery before showing the man who seems impressed with my ability to hold the camera steady. 'It's more difficult here on the boat than on land,' I say, 'but I also use a fast shutter speed; otherwise, it would start to get quite blurred.'

'It's certainly a nice camera,' he says, 'quite professional.'

'Not really,' I say. 'I'm sure there's better than this.' He starts to nose around me and starts asking where I'm from. I tell him I'm stopping off at Dervaig at the moment, up with my niece. At this point, he seems quite interested and asks a bit about her. I tell him that my niece, Amy, is a bit like myself, but doesn't like going out in the water to catch the animals, so today I'm taking the trip on my own. He asks quite a lot about her, particularly what she looks like and I give him a description of Susan, something quite general. I don't want to look like I'm an investigator, detailing everybody to the last freckle on their face.

The boat isn't that big but you're able to go below deck where they have one of those Portaloos and it's with an excuse that I need the toilet that I make my way down. I hear the three of them laughing up above as I conduct a quick search below decks. There's nothing unusual, some drinks sitting around to obviously sell to punters, the basic sort of life-saving equipment you would expect, and I can hear the engine room beyond. There's, however, one fixed container at the side that has a lock on it—everything else seeming to have free access except for this. I make a note of it as I go to the bathroom. I say bathroom but really, it's a cupboard with a toilet in it and as the boat rolls about, it's not that easy to do your business.

When I get back up on deck, I ask if there's any chance of some coffee and Digsy gets sent off to make some. Over the next hour, I drink three cups much to the amazement of the crew. As we're heading back up towards Tobermory, I tell them I need the bathroom and head back down below but this time holding my bladder tight, I take out my lock-pick and quickly work the lock. It's a lock you could buy in a hardware store, it

CHAPTER SIX

really isn't difficult at all, but it still takes me a minute working with my single hand to get it open. At one point I hear John shout out 'Are you all right?' and I tell him I'm fine, it's just that I need to do a number two rather than number one.

With the lock open, I quickly open the container and see a lot of bags inside, large and small. I'm not sure what the large ones are for yet, but some of the smaller ones I see are similar to those the drugs were packaged up in. I reach down, take one, close the container and snap the lock shut as I hear footsteps coming down from above. I turn around half pretending to pull up my zipper, the bag tucked away inside my hand.

'You all right?' says John, eyeing me suspiciously.

'I'm fine,' I say.

'We're only about ten minutes out,' he says, 'and we will be dropping you off, just in case you want to get any shots of the harbour as we pull in.'

I nod and say, 'Good idea', brush past him, and make my way up onto the deck. Once there, I do as he suggests, and I take photographs of the coloured houses as we come in. I see Digsy getting sent down to below as John stands by and then jumps onto the harbour side to tie the boat up. Andrew asked how I did and I tell him the scenery was nice. I caught a couple of birds but frankly, I might need to go out again on another day. He hands me a card, showing the boat trips. I say I'll be in touch and John says to me to bring my niece with me next time. I tell him I probably will.

I don't know how I feel about Susan playing that sort of card, flirting with someone to get information; she's not been prepped for it and it suddenly dawned on me what an asset I have in her. These three guys would never be interested in anything I'm doing but bring somebody like Susan on board at their age and they'll be hopping around to impress.

I shake hands with Andrew, jump onto the quayside and find a nearby pub. There's a fire in the corner and I draw up a chair and sit beside it as the barmaid brings me a pot of tea. I order some food because once again I'm starting to shake with a bit of hunger and cold.

Drawing out my mobile, I ring Susan but I can't get anywhere. Maybe she's out of signal. Still, I should be able to find her tonight and we can catch up on where we're at. I head back out and see the boat's still there with Andrew and his crew tightening things up. I keep my distance and follow them when they leave the quayside, watching as they disappear **down a** backstreet and pick up a car. I clock the colour—thankfully, it's burgundy, and the number plate registers with me. It's a small Beetle—won't be difficult to spot but I still run back to my own car and catch it pulling out of Tobermory.

We route back along the road that I came originally through Dervaig and out towards Calgary Bay. We pass by it and a short distance later I see the Beetle stop at a house. It's an old bungalow and all three of them get out. I park the car up about half a mile down the road and then trace my way back, running across the moor, and I'm able to hide behind a couple of trees, looking at the house.

Over the next hour, nobody comes out and I'm convinced this is where they live. I feel the shivers come again in the cold. Realizing that I may be at the end of my tether, I head back to the hotel to grab yet another shower. Susan is not back and it's now coming near to teatime so I get myself a bite to eat. It's about three hours later when I'm in my bed that I'm rudely awoken by my phone.

I pick it up to hear Maggie's voice and as much as I'm

CHAPTER SIX

desperate to be with the woman, I really don't want to talk. She takes the hint, simply asking if I'm all right and not going on about her day. I tell her I'll speak to her tomorrow and promise I'll give her some time but given the fact that I'm planning to go out tonight, that may not be the case. As I put the phone down and think about getting another ten minutes' sleep, there is a knock on the door and without being told, Susan bursts in. 'Hey, Paddy,' she says, 'wait till you see what I've found!'

Chapter Seven

Despite having slept rough for the past few nights, I feel the need to do it again but this time not on Gometra; this time I will do it outside the house of the crew of the *Sandra Jane*. I'm not quite sure what to make of Andrew, Digsy, and John as they don't seem to be the run-of-the-mill smugglers or drug runners but they obviously have something going on and it looks like it could have to do with Keir. Surely, it can't be a coincidence that where his body was found, people might seem to be hiding, smuggling things. It's certainly worth more than a little investigation and with that in mind, I decide we need to watch the house. Susan's had a good couple of days tracking round Mull and finding a number of the sites in the photographs of Keir Matheson and as we now sit in the car, in the last few hours of daylight, watching the house of the *Sandra Jane* crew, she takes me through her findings.

I take a drink of tea from the flask we have sitting between us as Susan leans over, holding her tablet and spinning through the photographs.

'A lot of them are from around here,' she tells me. 'That's Calgary Bay, there's Gometra; as you can see, there's lots of birds, lots of wildlife.' As Susan flicks through the photographs, I see small spiders, plenty of our feathered friends, even the odd

CHAPTER SEVEN

rabbit running around. We have countryside with sheep, the dawn breaking over hillsides. There's even the odd night shot, the moon slicking down, sending its light like some space-age melodrama across a rippling sea. Wherever he was or wasn't, he certainly had some idea how to handle a camera and I wonder how much tutelage he got from Jack Doolan.

'Some of these other beaches, Paddy, I managed to find them. They are up north of Dervaig, a little bit out of the way and you have to walk to them. There's no cars or tracks, not even a short path up to it—it's literally a walk.'

'Or a boat ride,' I say. 'You can always take a boat round, something nice and simple, beach it up. It would be very out of the way for someone.'

She looks at me, 'I didn't think of that. It'd be kind of remote,' she said. 'To be honest, I find them quite romantic. I could see myself sitting there sunning myself, some bronzed hunk by my side, bringing me champagne and caviar, looking after my every need. In fact, if it had been summer, I might have spent an hour or two out there.'

I raise an eyebrow at her and she smiles back. 'Not on my time, you wouldn't,' I say. 'I'm paying you—you don't go sunbathing while you're on the job and with your white skin, you'll burn in no time.'

'Not with the sun round here, especially not at this time of the year; it's blooming freezing at those beaches.'

'But they are secluded. Did you get a chance to work out where he took the photographs from on those beaches?' I ask her.

'What do you mean?' she says.

'Look at the photographs on those other beaches,' I say. 'You go to Calgary Bay, he's taken photographs from the middle of the beach; he's taken them all over. There's nothing that says he can't be taking a photograph from a place. Those other pictures, all the photographs are from the side. Look at that one there,' I point at her tablet. 'Blow that one up!' She puts her thumb and her finger down, moves them apart and the screen increases in size. 'There's two figures on that beach, very distant—I can't make much of them out at all.'

'Maybe that's what ruined the shot,' she says.

'Hardly! Something's not right with those photographs; it's almost like there should be more. Count up the photographs of the different places, make a note of the different areas, and see what numbers you come up with.'

'What, right now?'

'Yes,' I say, 'right now. Where else are you going?'

Susan takes the tablet back and gets to work while I sit back in my seat feeling my shoulders. They are tired and aching and it's come from several nights sleeping rough. I may do the same again tonight but it's not going to be with a tent over my head. The car is facing away from the house where the crew of the *Sandra Jane* took their car. I'm guessing it's their house, a little strange to have the three lads living together but it's not unheard of. I'm looking in the rear-view mirror at the house and nobody's come in or out for at least an hour. Darkness is beginning to fall but I'm waiting for the full cover before I can sneak out and have a good look around the house. I may not get inside but at least I can listen at windows and try and find out what's going on. We have our black outfits in the boot, ready to get changed soon but we'll move the car before we do that. At the moment, we just look like a couple of tourists staring out at the sea taking in the falling sun, but if we leave the car here at night, it's too easily exposed and too easy to

CHAPTER SEVEN

have people point the finger and say 'what the heck are they doing?'

'You're right, Paddy' says Susan. 'There's distinctly less number of those beaches than there is of others in photographs. If you look at Calgary Bay and compare that to this beach,' she said, 'there's a quarter of the photographs and this other beach has got even less. I don't understand what that means,' she says. 'Does he just not like that beach?'

'Or did someone not like what he was shooting?' I take another sip of tea, chew it round my mouth. 'If we reckon who got access to his photographs, we could find out who possibly deleted some.'

'Maybe they didn't delete them at all, maybe they just took them for their own thing, or maybe there's something on it that they didn't like.'

'Very likely but who's the first person we could look at?' I pose this question to the air, seeing if she'll grab.

'Jack Doolan! He was the one teaching him all about photography—he's the one who would have seen all the photographs, surely,' says Susan.

I nod. 'And that means we need to get inside Jack Doolan's house, but not tonight. We're following this lead tonight. The other problem is if things don't go well, I may need Hans to help. I don't have it as expertise to find out what's been deleted and what hasn't, if it's been deleted at all.'

We wait another hour until the sun is fully descended before I drive the car off a short distance down the road and park it up down a track. The car is hidden by a number of trees and getting out, we change. One of the things I've noticed on this trip is how the relationship between myself and Susan has become a more professional one. In changing, we don't blink an eye at each other and that mutual attraction on our first meeting seems to have died off. It may have something to do with the fact that I'm dating her mother but whatever, it's a good thing.

Once we've both put on our clothing and covered our faces with black balaclavas, we grab a small bag and make our way through the fields of moorland, towards the house. It's fairly open with a couple of trees around it, which is why I've waited until night-time to make an approach. During the day, we'd be seen quite easily. As we get nearer, I make sure Susan's staying close by as she's still very green in these things. But she's not making a sound, looking only for my hand signals, and, in fairness, she's got an exceptionally light step.

As we approach the house, we manage to half run and crouch off to the side of it. It's a small bungalow with a tired whitewash on the outside which is not good to stand against given our black clothing, so I move us round towards a shed at the back which is brown and beginning to fall apart. There are several lights on in the house and I can see Andrew, the boat skipper, moving about the kitchen. He's swigging from a bottle of beer, turning around and talking to someone. After a few minutes, he leaves the kitchen and comes out the rear door heading towards the shed we're stood beside.

I quickly spin around, and Susan and I creep to the rear of the shed, listening carefully. I hear his feet crunch across the stone driveway that swings around the rear of the house. He's coming directly for the shed and my heart begins to tighten. I remove a small club from my jacket ready to give him a tap on the head in case he sees us but hopefully, he's not coming our direction. My ears prick up and I hear the door of the shed being opened and he steps inside. But there's more crunching

CHAPTER SEVEN

of feet across the driveway and I hear a second person enter the shed and the door's then closed.

'I think it's time we talked about this properly.' It's Andrew's voice and I wait to hear who else is in there.

'You can't be serious about Digsy; you can't seriously think he did it.' It's John, the man with the black beard. That makes sense to me as these two seem to be the bosses on the boat, Digsy being more of a cabin boy.

'All I know is that Keir ends up dead right at the place where we keep the stuff. We're bloody lucky nobody found it, and I mean what happened to him? He was out there with not a stitch on.'

'We have to be careful,' says John. 'We've nearly got enough money stashed away.'

'But we need to get it soon. We said the supply is running low and if we don't give it to them, they're going to kick off about it. You know we're still short. Another couple of runs would do it.'

'But he knows, he knows someone's taking it, he just doesn't know who. If he finds out it's us, we'll be stuck in Gometra as well.'

'It'd be a bit easier if we knew who he was. It's not like we've seen her in a while; we could do with that, we could do with knowing it's still okay, it's still going in the same place.'

'What?' says Andrew. 'You think she's going to come round here, just pop in, and say hello to us, check if everything's all right. It's not that easy to get hold of her; he sees her; he's watching her all the time.'

'But she'll be back for her cut, that's one thing you can be sure of.'

'We can't be the only people she's playing in this—she's too sophisticated for that, too good a mover.'

'But we don't want to go too far,' says John. 'I say we get another couple deliveries, another month at the most, and then we get out; we go, just sink the boat somewhere, pretend we drowned, get out. Something simple, then we can head off to Australia. By that time, we should be able to afford something, something sensible out there. Won't have to work again, can take our holidays somewhere nice, might even get a woman like her with me.'

Andrew laughs, 'What's a woman like her going to do with you?'

'When I've got enough money,' says John, 'they'll flock to me. Women who look like that don't care what the man looks like, especially if they chase the money.'

'And what of Digsy?' he says. 'I mean Keir's dead. I always wondered what we'd do with him but Digsy, I'm not sure he would keep his mouth shut when he gets money. What do we do with him?'

'Depending on how much he knows, we could drop him in it. He'd take care of it for us then; we wouldn't have to get our hands dirty.'

'Seriously,' says Andrew, 'Digsy might talk, they could torture stuff out of him, find out who we are, then they'd come after us. At the moment he knows nothing.'

'Don't be stupid,' says John. 'She's already our link—we should get rid of her as well.'

'How? How are we going to get rid of her; she's smarter than that? We could just toss Digsy over the boat when we're out one day, nobody would be any the wiser. It's not like anybody knows he's up here. He was only a man on the street, someone sleeping rough and homeless, we don't even know his real name. The guy is just delighted he's got food in his belly; the idea he's going to get a bit of money is what's keeping him going. Keir was different—that's the problem when you photograph stuff. The poor bugger. I wonder what they did to him beforehand—never found out what the body looked like.'

'So, are we agreed then?' says Andrew. 'Another month, a couple more runs, then we end it; we end Digsy, then we will take a look at what we can do with her.'

'Maybe she'd run with us for a while,' says John, 'I'd like a piece of that.'

'We'd all like a piece of that,' says Andrew and with that, one of them crunches his way back over towards the main house. A few minutes later, the second one retires. I thought I was going to have to go inside and do a lot more work, but this has been gold. I doubt they're going to go anywhere tonight. We might have to do more of a stakeout on them which is going to be a good job for Susan to do at a distance. I signal to her that we need to disappear back to the car. We stalk back across the field to where we've left the car and change back into our normal clothing. Driving back to the hotel, I can see Susan's face pumped up and excited.

'What is it they are into then?' she says. 'What are they smuggling about that's not even theirs?'

But my face is more serious. 'Indeed,' I say, 'and whoever's stuff they are taking, took Keir Matheson and killed him, no hesitation, left him as an open reminder for those who are messing about.'

'You're telling me I have to be careful, aren't you?' she says.

'Always,' I say, 'always be careful until you know who you're dealing with. This is obviously some sort of a player, so we take it easy—we don't mess about. I'm going to put you on watch with these guys, nothing too close, just keeping an eye where they go, when they're doing things. Get yourself a sketchbook and start drawing the wildlife and the plants around here and if anyone asks you or they catch you remember, you're my niece. Be a little strange, one of those quiet girls who doesn't talk to people. That way they'll think you're harmless.'

'So, what do we do now then?' she says. 'I take it I'm doing that tomorrow.'

'First thing, five a.m., you're going to be out there,' I say, 'and tomorrow I'm going to get ourselves some photographs. I'm going to find out where the rest of the photographs Keir took have gone but for now we head back, get some food, and we get to bed.'

'You don't fancy a couple of drinks, Paddy, before you go to bed? I don't even feel tired yet. It's not even ten.'

'Nope, I've slept in a tent in the middle of nowhere and been up half the night for the last lot of days and who knows how many more nights we're going to be up, so I am going to sleep, and you are on curfew, too.'

Susan smiles and laughs, 'You're stricter than my bloody mum—you know that?'

Chapter Eight

I didn't quite go straight to sleep last night but spent a lot of time talking to Hans. My technology man, Hans Weber, was a thief and not a bad one, but he dealt a lot with technology and stealing things that were stored on computers—disk drives, data, all sorts of things like that. Breaking into systems was his speciality until one day, I was involved in catching him, turning him around, and putting him back on a better path. So, he's pretty grateful to me and when he gets a call from his favourite one-armed former policeman, he always is ready to help. In the past, I've had him come along with me to break into places but now the technology gets better and better and he's able to direct me from a distance.

He tells me that if I can get in and get access to the computers, tablets, or whatever else people have in the Doolan household, that he can investigate the hard drives and cards, then clean it up and leave no computer trace. I don't know how that's done; all I know is I have to stick certain things into the sides of certain computers with them being switched on at times. Hopefully, the Doolans are the sort of people who don't switch devices off, making it much easier, but we'll see.

With the possibility of the boys being on the move, I saw Susan off just before five o'clock this morning. She, thankfully, did get a good night's sleep but she still looked bleary eyed. All she has to do today is simply watch them from a distance, keep an eye on their house. If they move or go anywhere, she's to ring me and I'm going to come with a car. I won't be that far away but it is a risk. Either way, we'll be able to trace them at some point. They'll be back in the house or round the boat and I doubt in daylight that they're going to move anything about. So, my key objective for today is to find out about those photographs.

It's ten o'clock before I leave the hotel, having breakfasted well and sorted out my gadgets into a little rucksack that I throw over my shoulder. It's not always easy to break into somewhere in the daylight, but I'm hoping with where we are, it's not going to be like a city where every darn house you go to has cameras.

Doolan's house was located behind a lot of trees and with this in mind, I drive the car and stop well short, parking it off the road to the side in a tourist car park. From here I'll walk along the road before diving behind a hedge as I get closer and hiding out in the trees that surround the house. About eleven o'clock, I see Jack Doolan and he's packing up lots of camera gear into the car. I can't see anyone else in the house at the moment. Skirting around through the trees, I look at all sides before concluding that there's a high percentage chance that nobody else is in. Doolan drives off and I believe he could be away for a while, given the number of cameras that he's put into his boot; maybe he's doing a shoot somewhere. Hopefully, it will be for a couple of hours at least.

I run up to the back door and try it, finding it open straight-away. You'd think people would lock their doors here or maybe it's so remote, he doesn't bother. It's then I also think maybe it's

CHAPTER EIGHT

because he's expecting someone to come back. As the thought enters my head, I hear feet outside. I duck, go in the kitchen, scrambling underneath a table at the side. Ten seconds later the back door opens, and I see a pair of legs and shorts, with some running shoes. The person is breathing heavily but it's a female pair of legs, so I guess it's Annie Doolan back from a run. I had hoped she'd made her way down to London for a while but clearly that isn't the case.

The worst thing to do at the moment is panic and try and move out of the way. Instead, I take my balaclava and slowly put it on my head in case I'm discovered. Of course, I've only got one arm so the disguise isn't great but if it comes to it, I'll see if I could throw her a punch and knock her out before running off. Maybe she won't have seen the lack of an arm. Who knows?

But like I said, the main thing to do now is not panic. The legs go back and forward as she seems to take drinks of water like it's going out of fashion. She then leaves the kitchen and I hear her go upstairs. Stepping out from under the table, I have a quick hunt around the lower floor of the house. There's an ornate dining room next to the kitchen which then leads through to a large sitting room. Everything's done with style and all is neat and packed away. Photographs line the walls, possibly taken by Doolan but there's one of Annie receiving some sort of award from medical-type people. I drift past a modern suite, open a door out to the hallway, and listen up the stairs.

Annie's singing and it's possibly coming from her bedroom or somewhere so I hold on downstairs looking around to see if I can see any computers. But the ground floor seems purely for pleasure—there's no office or study. Even when I check the conservatory at the back, there's no tablets or phones lying around.

I wait at the bottom of the stairs, seeing if she'll come back down but then hear a shower running. With that, I glide up the stairs, quickly as I can, and hear the bathroom door shut. Annie is one of those vocal people who seems to talk to themselves when no one's about. She's telling herself what a good run it was, how to relax, then she's standing in front of a mirror telling somebody that they'd love to get their hands on this body—you get all sorts when you do this sort of work—and I hear her step inside the shower, telling her shoulders how good that feels.

Upstairs, there's a shower room, three bedrooms and a study. I do a quick scan, inside of a minute, and I find the only devices to be in the study, just two computers—a his and hers by the looks of it—and I wonder which one to try first. They are both on and so I take the dongle from my backpack and stick it into one. The screen comes on and it's clearly Annie's as there seem to be a number of medical files all with the labels that would suggest diseases and ailments. I pull the dongle back out and stick it into the other computer and here I see programs that indicate graphic work, a manipulation of pictures. I receive a text telling me that Hans is on it. I watch the screen go dark.

The shower is still running and Annie Doolan is singing now and in fairness, she can hold a note but something's bothering me. If this is where Jack Doolan works, it seems weird that he just has a single computer; surely there's somewhere else or maybe I've missed something. I wonder if there's a basement. If he were an old-style photographer, a basement would work for him. I make my way quickly downstairs and search around the ground floor until I find a door that looks like it leads to

CHAPTER EIGHT

the underside of the stairs. It's locked . . . with a padlock as well.

I can easily break it and I reckon that's what I'll do when I get a text from Hans which tells me he's ready. I run back up the stairs and as I enter the office, my hairs go on end as I hear the shower finish. I grab the dongle ready to sprint back downstairs while Annie Doolan dries herself, but I hear the door open. Desperately, I look around the room, two desks, sofa in the corner, and I jump behind the sofa. There's not an awful lot of space, and I lie down as I hear footsteps enter the room. I can see a couple of inches, enough to notice somebody walk in and I guess Annie Doolan must only have a towel around her head given the bare backside that walked past me. The things people do in their houses when they think they're alone always amazes me, especially if she leaves the back door open. Anyone could be in here, anyone like me.

I hear her tut for a bit and then she disappears off, possibly into the bedroom. I come out from behind the sofa, grab the dongle, sticking it in the pack behind me. When I go to the door from the study, I can see that the door of the bedroom is also open. Without hesitating, I run across the landing and make my way quickly down the stairs. At the bottom, I start fumbling about with the under-stairs' lock and it takes me a minute to break it open. Single-handed is always slow.

As I'm completing the work, I hear Annie coming down the stairs, I lean back inside against the door underneath the stairs and she walks past me wearing a white dress, enters into the kitchen, and I follow her at a distance to see what she's doing. Making herself a cup of tea, she also grabs some bread, something from the fridge and concocts a sandwich before walking through the dining room and into the lounge, where she puts on the TV. I find it quite funny that she's sitting down to watch a program about hospitals, a fictional one at that. Surely, she must know better but taking the chance, I make my way back to the door that leads under the stairs, open it, close it over and flick on a light switch beside me.

Steps descend into a basement and I see a proper set of photography tools. A lot of it is old style, chemical stains and all those old ways of producing photographs, as well as another computer. I make straight for the computer, stick the dongle in and await a text. Sure enough, I get one and then I turn to see what else I can find. I notice a large number of photographs, colour ones, sitting out on a table beyond where the chemical basins are, my breath taken away as I look at some of the photographs.

There's a dark-haired woman, hair down to her shoulders with an all-over tan. I can tell this because there's nothing preventing me from seeing the whole tan. The photographs are very professional, very artistic, and she appears to be standing on a beach, one which I think I've seen recently. When I say they're artistic, the most of them are but one or two are a little more graphic. I have to say any man looking at these would be quite taken by them because she looks like one of those models. Certainly, someone blessed with a figure that you usually only see in magazines and books. I take out my small camera and start photographing some of the pictures, not for my own personal use but because I want to know who she is. I search through some filing cabinets and note that there are now hundreds of photographs of the same woman; sometimes she's wearing some scanty clothing, other times not, but she certainly doesn't look forced and seems to be quite enjoying parading around these beaches. One thing I notice in

CHAPTER EIGHT

the photographs is that they appear to be at different times of year but always the same beaches, never anywhere else. Could it be that this is being done on the quiet? Why is he padlocking his office when his wife stays here?

It's been ten minutes and I get a text. Hans has finished again and so I take out the dongle, put it in the backpack, preparing to leave. I've seen plenty of photographs and I make my way back up the stairs, flick off the light switch, close the door behind me and lock up. I take a peek in to see what Annie Doolan is up to and I see her lying fast asleep on the couch, the TV still blaring. I make my way back out through the kitchen, and route across the field back to my car.

There has been no contact from Susan, so I head back to the hotel and grab a spot of lunch, then make my way back up to my room. I take out my laptop where Hans has emailed me some files through. I feel a bit funny, sitting in my room looking at these pictures, a little bit on the dirty side but this is work and I'm studying more than the central figure. I see again those beaches and comparing them with some of the photographs that Susan took, I realize that they are the same beaches, the ones that Keir had taken photographs of. But then I see some photographs with Jack Doolan in them, holding a camera in front of the woman, the photographs taken from a distance. There are a number of these and then there's a large number of photographs where the woman seems different, not so professional, less model-like, more candid, more relaxed. I see a picnic laid out on the beach as well, I see her swimming and then there's photographs of Keir photographing her, all shot from a distance with a longer lens.

My mind's racing now. Keir had been with her, but also Doolan was photographing her. Did Doolan introduce him to her? Did he find her on his own? Did he find Doolan's photographs of her? The man's obviously quite precious about them and I wonder if his wife knows. Once again, there's more questions but I also need to know who this woman is. If she's local to the area and a model, we should be able to find her. Is she doing this stuff for pay? Is she a bored lonely housewife? Is she some professional who likes to do these on the side? More questions.

I think we could do with watching Mr Doolan and where he goes to see if he meets her as well. This is annoying because we're starting to get stretched and I wonder how many suspects I'm going to end up watching. For now, I switch off the laptop, pick up my phone and give Maggie a call. She wonders why I'm ringing her in the middle of the day as she's working in the hospital but to be honest with you, after sitting at that laptop and looking through those photographs, I need something to take my mind off because that woman's got the eyes, not just the body . . . and I wonder what she did with Keir and what part got him killed.

Chapter Nine

When I meet up with Susan that night, she has little to tell me. I've got quite a bit to tell her, but I decide not to bring the laptop down to dinner as some of these pictures may be a little bit too disturbing for the locals. Instead, after dinner, up in my room, I take her through what I found out in Doolan's house. It's a little bit awkward showing these sorts of things to a teenage girl and I can see her jump a little when she sees the first of the pictures and get a little bit more uncomfortable when she sees some of the more risqué ones. I don't linger and close down the laptop once she's seen a few of them.

'So, you can see what he's been up to,' I say. 'We need to find the girl so I'm going to track him for a few days and see where he goes. I want you to stay watching the boys in the boat.'

She nods. 'Paddy, open it up again because I recognize those beaches.' Obediently, I open up the laptop and she slides in front of me, making her way through the photographs. She shows an impressive, professional edge as she calmly turns to me pointing out different ones and saying where they are on the map. She looks through the date stamp on each of the photographs.

'Keir was doing these photographs right up until he died,' she says. 'It makes me wonder what's going on here. We've seen people moving what we believe could be drugs about and yes, I understand that could be a good reason for murder, but have you thought of the possibility that Keir may have been taking these photographs without Doolan's knowledge?'

'That occurred to me, which is one reason why I need to speak to the young woman in these photographs, find out what's the deal with her but Doolan seems to be taking an awful lot of photographs of her himself. If you notice, quite a few of them are artistic; they're not all more' . . . *here is where I struggle to find the words* . . . 'medical?'

Susan laughs. 'Just wait till I tell my mom you've been looking at dirty photographs without her.' She punches my arm and I give her a look of 'Don't you dare.' I sometimes wonder what Maggie would think of what I do, the things I end up looking at. It's certainly not all glamour in this business although I could guess you could say that these photographs are.

The following morning, Susan's up early again, out of the hotel by five, to keep an eye on her sailing boys. I'm not far behind her and by six o'clock, I'm sat outside the Doolans. One thing that does puzzle me, as I sit low down in a hedge row, unseen by all and sundry, is why keep the cupboard locked? Why's all his photography locked away from his wife? Does it mean there was more to these photographs than simple modelling and just who is this woman? I decide to make a phone call and find out just how much Mrs Doolan knows.

'Hello, Doolan residence,' says a female voice picking up the receiver.

'Hello, this is Mr Jones, making an inquiry for Doolan photography.'

'Ah, okay. I'm sorry, my husband's just in the shower at the

CHAPTER NINE

moment. Can I help?'

'Oh, that's not a problem,' I say. 'I was just wondering if your husband does glamour photography.'

'My husband does a wide range of photography; it may be niche or not, what did you exactly mean by glamour photography?'

'Oh, it's just something that I wanted to do for my wife, she's always wanted to pose in that, you know, al fresco? And I was just wondering if your husband did that sort of photographs?'

'I'm not quite sure what you mean, sir.'

'I sort of mean, nudes, naked, that sort of photographs. It's just something my wife's always wanted to do and I was looking for someone discreet who could take them. I wasn't sure from your husband's website whether or not it was something he did.'

'Certainly not, I'm afraid,' she says. 'While everyone's entitled to their own lifestyle, it's not something we do here but thank you for your inquiry.'

'Oh, not a problem,' I say. 'Thank you for your time.'

So, she has no idea what he does, and frankly, he didn't seem to have any other photographs of that type so maybe this is a private arrangement. But of what sort, I don't know. I spend the day looking at the house because Doolan doesn't leave it. By half past four in the afternoon, I've given up for the day because the light will be going, and I see a car drive out. It's not Doolan's but it is quite flashy. It's a nippy Porsche and I see Annie Doolan in the front and so I follow her.

It's not difficult to tail her; she's probably not looking for anyone, but we end up in Tobermory. At this point, I decide to put my prosthetic on and walk down the street behind her as she disappears into a quiet pub. Retracing my steps back to the car, I put on a beard and a wig that changes my hair colour to a more-brown shade instead of the usual black. I'm not going to be too close to her, sitting at a distance. I make my way back to the pub to find her sitting at a corner on her own with large glass of wine. I sit up at the bar on the other side of the room and order a pint myself. Don't worry, it's alcohol free because you never know when you have to drive. It's embarrassing to get caught under the influence when you're in pursuit of someone.

She's looking around quite furtively, and I wonder what's on the go. It's then I see a sharply dressed woman in her forties enter the bar, smart black trousers and a waistcoat of colourful design on it. Her blonde hair seems to bounce as she walks right past me heading for the far end of the pub. She's got a jacket over her arm that she must have taken off pretty recently because it's cold out there and on her left hand, she carries a smart briefcase. I watch her sit down with Annie Doolan, who seems to be pouring her heart out to her with the woman simply nodding. At one point the briefcase is opened, and some photographs are shared. There's a signing of a piece of paper, who knows what, and after an hour, Annie Doolan leaves and the blonde woman continues to sit. I could tail Annie but I reckon she's probably going back to her house having concluded her business for the evening but I'd like to know who the other woman is although I do have very strong suspicions. In my game, you get to know the others, the competition.

Recently, there's been talk of a former cop starting up work on the west side of Scotland. She's been doing a lot of infidelity cases which is not unusual when you start. People always want to know about their spouses and it's kind of a bread and butter thing without getting your hands too messy or in somewhere

CHAPTER NINE

too dangerous but the problem is that if this woman is carrying out surveillance on Jack Doolan, then she may also support me carrying out surveillance on him. I'm going to have to really keep my wits about me; she's obviously been doing something so far as you don't hand over photographs without taking them somewhere and I wonder who's in them. I also wonder if this is a straight infidelity case or not.

I get up and walk past the blonde woman sitting at the far side of the pub and manage to snap a quick shot with my camera and in truth, for her age, she's looking very well. But she does have a scar on one side of her face—maybe that's what took her out of the business, the official business, not my one. Who knows? But what I do know is that I need to find out who exactly she is. Returning to the bar, I send the picture off to Martha and sit and calmly wait. I possibly would have gone up and flirted a couple of months ago before I met Maggie but I'm trying not to use any of that sort of tactic anymore, just makes it awkward when you have to go home and explain it, even more awkward if her daughter walks in—after all, she is working with me. It's about forty minutes later and I receive a message on my phone and as usual, Martha has come up with the goods.

Her name is Sarah Hunstanton, formerly of the Metropolitan Police who left after an incident where she lost a colleague and she was horribly disfigured. Apparently, after months of facial surgery, she's come back. I have to give it to whoever was doing the operations, they've done a heck of a job. I'm gazing down at a couple of photographs of her on the phone when I realize she's got up and walked towards the bar. I'm resting my prosthetic on the bar and I wonder if she's noticed it. It's not easy to make it look natural all the time. She's got a briefcase with her and her coat and plonks them on a chair that's two away from me and occupies the chair in the middle. The bartender comes over and she orders a gin and tonic before turning to me and asking if I want one.

'Well, that's truly kind of you,' I say, 'but I'm not accustomed to taking drinks thrust upon me by a good-looking woman without knowing her name.'

I wish I could say things a lot smoother but there you go. She turns to me, holds out her hand and says 'Sarah.' I shake hands with her,

'Paddy,' I say.

'Ah, an Irishman,' she says.

'Ulsterman,' I say. 'I'm from the North—maybe you can't tell that from the accent.'

She smiles, 'And so what brings you here?' she says.

She doesn't have that stereotypical English accent, not one from around the London area that sounds so strait-laced you heard it off the television. It's elsewhere and I'm trying to place it. There's a softness in the tone and then it comes to me. 'Business,' I say, 'what brings you up from Devon?'

She laughs. 'I haven't been in Devon in years,' she says, 'but it's a good spot—it is where I'm from.'

'Oh, really?' I say. 'Where have you been then?'

Smiling, she looks away for a moment, as if contemplating something before turning back. 'I used to work in London, but I had a few issues in getting back on my feet and so I'm up here doing a little bit of business myself.'

'Oh,' I say, 'what kind of work are you in?'

'Investigations,' she says.

I feign to look shocked. 'You're not investigating me, are you?' I ask.

CHAPTER NINE

Again, she laughs. 'No,' she says, 'not at all. I'm just stuck here for the evening and I thought that man looks like he could talk to someone—maybe I'll keep him company for a while.'

'By all means,' I say, 'especially if the woman's buying me drinks but it is to talk a while and keep company,' I say. 'Sorry for being forward but there's someone else at home.' She nods her head. 'That's just typical,' she says. 'I always manage to pick them. A lot of men struggle and yet you haven't seemed to look once at it.'

'At what?' I say.

'You're too kind,' and she turns her head so her scar is showing fully to me. It runs from her neck, right down across her cheek to her mouth.

'That must have been nasty,' I say, 'but it hardly defines you.'

Again, she smiles. It's because I'm saying all the right things; whether or not she believes it, is up to her. In truth, it does ruin her face, you can't get away from that scar, not that it would bother me but it's always going to be there, a bit like my missing arm. People can talk about it being all right and all that but it's there. I carry it with me or rather I don't.

'So, what do you do yourself, Paddy?' she asks.

'I'm in investigations too,' I say, 'but it's okay. I'm not investigating you either.' She laughs and we sit for the next half an hour, talking idly about nothing. I detect the loneliness in the woman and maybe she is up here after living most of her life down in London. It's not easy. I know this because I've been there, out on my own trying to grab a bit of company where you can. We're chatting away when Susan walks into the pub. I thought it likely she could be around the Tobermory area because that's where the boys' boat is, but it does take me a little by surprise and I think my face might show it. Susan walks up beside me, takes a good hard stare at Sarah, and then looks at me quizzically.

'Ah,' says Sarah, 'this must be the woman at home. You've done well for yourself there, Paddy,' she says in a cheeky turn of phrase.

'And who's this?' says Susan. There's a little bit of misconstruing going on here and Susan's obviously very annoyed that I'm talking to another woman without her mother present. But I have nothing to be afraid of, or ashamed of.

'Susan, meet Sarah, she's an investigator as well. We have just met tonight and we're just killing time. Sarah, meet Susan, she's not the woman at home.'

Susan looks a little shocked, then turns around to Sarah and says, 'Do you think I'd go out with this fossil?' I laugh because I know she tried to.

'Susan's my associate,' I explain, 'and also the daughter of the woman at home.'

Sarah laughs, 'I can see why she seemed a little shocked when you were speaking to me. 'Don't worry,' she says, 'we're only chatting. I'm not after this fossil as you so admirably call him.'

I buy Susan a drink and we spend the next half an hour chatting with Sarah. We are talking about nothing important, simply passing the time. Once I get back to the car and alone with Susan, I explain exactly who Sarah Hunstanton is and why she needs to be wary of her.

'She's just investigating and if she sees you about or asking questions, just tell her that you're on a case but do not mention the Doolans. Annie Doolan is for some reason investigating her husband. I can see that's a jump but it's the most obvious one, so keep an eye out,' I say, 'in case you're being followed but if you're on the boys on the boat, I doubt they will be a problem. I just have to watch that I'm not being tailed myself.'

'What happened to her face?' says Susan. I turn and look at her and point to the arm with the prosthetic. 'This is the job you're in,' I say; 'happens to us all, happens to us all. It's just a pity it happened to her face. My arm was never that good looking.'

Chapter Ten

The following morning everyone's on the move early. Once again at six o'clock, I'm sat outside the Doolans'. I've parked the car further along the road this time, made my way to the fields and the hedges to sit down in the dark before the day begins. Mrs Doolan is off early. Maybe she's off to London, but she's out of the house by seven o'clock, taking that cracking little Porsche with her. As I'm bored, I scan around the house looking to see if Doolan's doing anything, but he doesn't stir until ten.

I've also managed to clock somebody else watching the house, Sarah Hunstanton, and in fairness, she's fairly good but not that good. She hasn't seen me and I'm going to keep it that way, but it could be interesting when it comes to tailing her. It's past midday before Doolan leaves the house and racing back to my car, I fall in line behind Sarah Hunstanton, who is driving at a distance to him. I could speed up, overtake and try and get behind Doolan himself but that would look obvious and so I trust Hunstanton's tracking techniques and ability to stay on the tail.

We head off to the northwest of Mull where Doolan parks up his car. Sarah drives past and parks up some distance away and I then join the charade by driving even further past and

CHAPTER TEN

parking up out of the way as well. I keep my distance as I see Doolan head across the moorland and Sarah behind him. She's just about keeping him in sight and it's all done extremely well, so I keep her just in sight and follow.

Within an hour, we've reached the beach and it seems to be incredibly out of the way because he's got the large pack on his back, one with presumably all of his camera gear inside. Sarah goes around to one side of the cove where the man has stopped, able to see him without him looking back up to see her. I route to the other side of the cove to look down on them at the beach. I'm somewhere where I can keep Sarah in sight as well. For an hour, he sits taking out some sandwiches and a flask and having an ordinary lunch. The case and his camera come out and he seems to spot something. I'm not sure if it's a bird or what else but he's definitely got his eye on something.

One thing I notice about the way the cove is situated is if standing on one side of it, it would be difficult to see you from the shore. There's certainly plenty of spaces where you could have a liaison without being spotted from a distance. It's about two o'clock when there's a putt of a small boat arriving. There are only two people on board and it's one of those hard-hulled RIBs, with a woman at the front and a man piloting the boat at the rear. It **motors** round, pulls up on the front of the beach so the woman is able to jump out into the water. Without looking back, she simply walks to shore, dressed in a simple pair of shorts and a gown over her top. It's more than a little strange and I watch the boat pull away without a second thought.

The woman comes to shore and Doolan steps up to greet her. Through my binoculars I recognize her; she's the woman from the photographs and frankly, she doesn't look that happy. There's no embrace between them, nothing at all. He doesn't offer her a drink or any of his sandwiches, instead pointing over to a part of the bay which is closer to Sarah Hunstanton than it is to me. I don't move because I can see anything I need to see from here, but I notice Sarah start to edge her way round.

The woman in question is very matter of fact as she simply removes all of her clothing, allows herself to be directed into various poses by Doolan and in fairness, I try to only watch what I have to as there's not a lot to tell—she's here, he's taking pictures. Sarah Hunstanton, on the other hand, has moved around and with her camera, is taking photographs of Doolan. The man's taking a lot of heat at the moment caught out in what seems to be a very strange facade. Why come all the way here to take photographs with someone who doesn't even seem to be your lover?

They change positions and the woman's now got her back to me and so I train in with the binoculars on Doolan's face. There's a leer to it and he doesn't look like a professional cameraman; rather he just seems to be enjoying it in a way that isn't detached. It takes about three hours before the boat comes back for the woman. She simply slips back into shorts, wraps her gown around her, walks back through the surf and gets into the boat. She's fully tanned and I think she has an Asian tinge to her now; there's something of that background in her face. She also has that smooth supple shape that most Asians manage and less the large curves that come with us white European settlers.

The boat disappears and I try to see it from my position, scrabbling off to the side as best I can without being seen. I think it goes into Tobermory, but I can't be definite and so I wait for Doolan to come back up from the beach and head back to his car. Sarah Hunstanton follows and together the parade

CHAPTER TEN

takes place until Doolan is back in his house and me and Sarah are outside watching from a distance.

That night at dinner in the hotel, Susan tells me a story. The boys she was watching had simply gone out on the boat again, taking a passenger with them, touring around and then coming back in. There seems to be extraordinarily little movement from them in terms of the secret stash they have. Given this information, I decide we spend another day in surveillance of our respective targets. I think Susan's getting quite bored with it now and she's realizing that it's not all glamour in my job, not so much running around and hiding from bad people as it's keeping an eye on people not doing a lot.

The following morning, I'm up early and I'm pleased to say that Sarah Hunstanton is too, settled in her perch before I've even got there. But this morning is different and Doolan comes out from his house for a walk by eight o'clock and together the two of us track him, me keeping a distance from her, until he walks the short distance over to Calgary Bay. He takes a stroll around the beach and I see Susan walking along with her shoes off paddling in the waves trying to be close but inconspicuous. In fairness she's probably done a good job. I prefer to stay further back and keep the binoculars on them both.

Doolan makes his way back off the bay, which is a crescent shape and has a large amount of grassland before you get back to the road. Walking across that grassland, he crosses the road and makes his way over to what looks like a cemetery. He stands in front of several gravestones and takes some photographs. I count the number round from the side, it's three and it's two from the back row, and I walk back with Doolan as he makes it to his house. Sitting in my perch, I then notice that Sarah Hunstanton has now come back as well. No doubt she was at the graves, taking close-up photographs of them but I'll do that on my way back or I might even do it in the dark.

Doolan goes out in the afternoon into Tobermory but all he does is pick up some groceries and then make his way back to his house again. The day is overcast, unlike yesterday, and while I wouldn't say it was warm, it was at least more pleasant than yesterday for standing around posing.

I've always thought there would be a lot more to taking pictures, the makeup, the lighting, but none of that seemed to be there. So, I'm wondering just exactly what sort of photographs these are and who they're for, I'll need to track the girl and find out where she lives. To do this, I'll need to know the next time they're shooting and so I wait later on that evening, telling Susan I'll be back to the hotel at a much later time.

Doolan goes to bed at close to midnight and it's then I make my way in the dark to his door. It's not a difficult lock to pick but he has locked the door. Once inside the kitchen, I listen for any sound in the house and I can hear some light snoring from upstairs. I reckon what he won't do is keep anything of this business outside of the locked cupboard that heads to the basement under the stairs so that's where I head directly, unlocking the fastening with my lock picks and descend the stairs.

I put the light on because at the end of the day, if he sees the lock off, he knows somebody's down there anyway, and I can get this done much quicker with some light about. I hunt around the desk looking for anything that gives any clues. There's nothing on the main table except some photographs which must have been taken today. There's a large A2 size print of the Asian woman and I try not to stare too long because it

CHAPTER TEN

is remarkably good.

Thankfully, she's not really my type and I remain professional sorting through the table, trying to find something that would indicate some sort of schedule. I break into the filing cabinets and underneath a collection of photographs, I find a small book. It has dates on the side, one of which corresponds to two days ago when we were all at the beach. There's simply the date, then there's the words 'Site Two' and the times, two to five, and an annotation that the weather will be okay. I look down to find another date which is tomorrow and the time eight o'clock at night until eleven. I didn't think about a night shoot or how to do that because surely that will involve a lot more equipment and lighting set up and it doesn't say 'Site Two' anymore. Instead it says 'NP'. Is that 'new place'? Is this a specific place? But I guess I'll have to track him to find out and I wonder if I'll be followed by Sarah Hunstanton.

I've got what I came for, so I tidy things back up to the way they were before I quickly back out, switching off the light and putting all the locks back. When I get back to my room in the hotel, it's one in the morning and I really just want to flop down on the bed. I'll leave a note for Susan to say that I am lying in and not to disturb me but to carry on with what she's doing. As I get changed there's a knock at the door, I put on my dressing gown and open it and Susan's standing there in her own dressing gown.

'How did it go, Paddy? Did you find anything?' I let her in and she sits down on the bed while I run through what's happened. I tell her I'm going to be out tomorrow night and hopefully, I'll have some information by then. She tells me that today the boys on the boat looked a lot more agitated and a couple of times they were shouting at Digsy although she couldn't tell from the distance she was at what it was about. I ask her whether they have spotted her yet and she says that one actually came over to talk to her but she said she was doing the photographs and kept pointing to the buildings in Tobermory, the many colours that change as you go along the bay. She thinks they were satisfied with that answer and that they came over more to try and chat her up than investigate what she was up to.

I'm a good employer and tell her to be careful and to keep the distance. But I don't know what else to do with her at the moment other than to keep her on this side of the investigation. Telling her I'll be about tomorrow but generally resting up because I think I might be out during the night, I also ask about taking pictures, how she would feel if she was transported to a bay on a boat. I point out how cool the woman was—she didn't look agitated, but neither was she happy. I want to see Susan's take on where the woman's coming from.

'I think she's being forced,' she says. 'There's something that means she has to do it and she can't get out of it so she's just getting on with it. You said there was no banter between them?'

'That's right,' I said, 'but he seemed to be leering a lot, enjoying it.'

'But wouldn't you?' said Susan.

'Well, in one sense, yes, but if I were the photographer, I wouldn't be showing it like that,' I say. 'Seems unprofessional.'

'Well,' says Susan, 'usually, he's got no assistant and no other gear with him. Maybe that's part of the deal; maybe they need to keep it on as quiet a level as possible. You gotta ask who wants these photographs, haven't you? I mean, he's being paid to produce them so does she have a lover?'

'But you said she looks like she's having to do it. Is it a lover or is it a pimp?'

I see Susan's shudder. 'That's horrible. I get if somebody wanted to do it for someone, I understand if they wanted to do it for themselves, but to make somebody go around like that, it's just horrible.'

I agree and tell her it's time to get off the bed. Unfortunately, I think she's beginning to understand some of the world we move in and I hope it's not something that will put her off her job because at the moment for a rookie, she's doing very well. As she goes out my door, she turns around and looks at me. 'Is everything like this, Paddy? Everything we've looked at so far, I mean. The last case, there was people playing around, people extorting making money out of people and now we come here and he's lying to his wife, she's investigating him, this girl has been forced to do who knows what and these boys are running around, and we've got a dead body that kicked it all off. Don't you get any nice cases?'

I nod my head. 'I'm sure there are some nice ones but they're over pretty quick and they don't pay well.' She looks back at me and it takes her a couple of seconds to realize that I'm joking. 'We work amongst the filth,' I say. 'Unfortunately, that's where the money is.' She bows her head a bit and I reach forward picking up her chin so she looks at me. 'Just make sure it's for you, this life,' I say; 'if it's not, it's fine and you can go anytime. Now, I spent my life investigating and seeing the bottom end of society. It's what I do but you've got years left, so give it a go but if it's not for you, just walk. I'm fine with that.'

She looks at me, nods her head and says 'Thanks, Paddy.' As I watch her disappear back into the door of her room, I do wonder if I should be encouraging her into this life. There's me with my missing arm, Sarah Hunstanton with a slash across her face, and I know countless other PIs that are just a mess in the mind. But as Maggie said to me, it's Susan's choice and she wouldn't take that away from her—so how can I?

Chapter Eleven

After taking some rest, I head back out for my nighttime observation of Doolan's liaison with the girl who comes to model. As I'm unsure of where it's going to be held, I do my usual routine of parking up near to his house and awaiting his departure. I'm sitting all prepped, waiting for the off, when I notice a black car pull up at the driveway to Doolan's house. Annie Doolan is not around, presumably having headed back to London for a few days and it's with interest I note the woman get out of the car and simply walk down the drive while the black car disappears. Before she can reach the front door, it's opened, and I see a smiling Doolan quickly look out before moving inside. The woman's left to walk into the house herself and close the door behind her.

That's a bit of a development so I make my way up to the house, leaning up close against the walls, trying to hear anything inside. It's fairly quiet and I wonder where exactly they've gone inside the house. With a woman coming to do provocative pictures like she does, would you take her to the bedroom, the kitchen? Surely not downstairs into his little hidey hole in the basement? I really don't know. And with Annie away, has Jack decided to rearrange the furniture? A strange curiosity inside me burns to see how he does the setup;

I also know it's not the reason for me being here. I know what he does with her; all I want is to follow her back to wherever she's coming from.

But this is different—usually they're on the beach and I wonder why he's suddenly taking this approach. I spin round the back of the house and look through to the kitchen but no one's there. I move on round to the next window looking in, but I can find no one. It's when I move to the front of the house that I realize the curtains are closed which stands to make sense because you wouldn't wander about in front of the window being seen by everyone.

And then I hear the rear door open and watch as Jack Doolan leads the woman across the rear path under some trees at the back. There's a large copse which is extremely sheltered and he's making his way with only a torch. I follow at a distance and arrive just in time to see them begin their work. The woman drops the gown she's in and almost immediately Doolan starts giving instructions. The copse itself is lit up by a number of lights coming from the side. I assume whoever enjoys these photographs wants some that have a night-time feel to them. I haven't got a clue why you'd want them like this or how you would actually start paying money to have this range of photographs? Must be an extremely strange fetish; surely you have the woman herself and that would be more than enough.

But I've learned over my time never to judge what people are doing, simply record it and try and work out their motives. If you start prejudicing what you're seeing, you start missing things—that's the trouble with investigative work, your mind has to go places that it normally wouldn't. The places that are very strange and sometimes extremely sick that people take theirs to.

CHAPTER ELEVEN

It's about two hours' worth of shooting before the woman's allowed to put her gown back on and together they make their way back into the house. I reckon she will be on the move soon, so I run back to my car and start driving up and down the road waiting for her transport to appear. Sure enough, about half an hour after she's finished, the black car appears again and parks at the end of the road. I drive past it, go as far as I can while keeping it in sight, switch off my headlights, turn around and park up into the side. Not the greatest idea but at least it keeps me dark rather than driving up and down several times where they can spot my car. The woman emerges pretty quickly and again, from the binoculars, I see no hint of a goodbye or a farewell. It's all very sterile, that is except for the face of Jack Doolan. He has that grin on again. There's a sort of leer that would creep a person out and I get the feeling he more than enjoys his job.

The car pulls off and I start to follow it, keeping at a good distance. We travel back through Dervaig before eventually cutting off onto a small track. It's at this point I don't take my car down because according to my map, this track doesn't really go anywhere. There's potentially some sort of building at the end. I'm gonna look ridiculous if I drive up in a car, only to find it stops at their house. What was I doing? Why was I going all the way down this track? Too easy to get caught like that.

I park my car up a little distance from the track's beginning, don my black gear and head out without my prosthetic. At the end of the day, it's too cumbersome to move around with. I have to walk about half a mile up the track before I start to see something that makes me very wary. There's a camera feed and a fence around a large house. It's got those iron gates and I can see a couple of men standing beside them. They're doing a good job of staying out of the way and you'd have to be looking for them to know that they're there but approaching anywhere, I'm always looking for anything that could cause me trouble.

I skirt round the house keeping a good distance from it, watching that fence. The camera appears to be only at the front gate but that might just be my oversight. I move round to the rear of the house and reckon I could jump the fence given enough of a start but at the rear there's a back gate which doesn't seem to have any cameras around it. I sneak up closer and realize it's padlocked with an old rusty padlock and a large rock put on the other side. The gate itself is a wooden frame but the wires of the fence seem to run across it and from the hum I'm hearing, I reckon I can get quite a shock off it.

Normally, an electric fence gives a shock that doesn't kill; it's there as a deterrent, whether for an animal or a person, but I'd rather test that with an animal or somebody else and not me. I take out my lockpick tools and reach through for the lock, being careful not to touch my arm on any of the wiring passing beside it and I have to put my face up extremely close to the fence to hold the lock in my teeth while I work on it with one hand. It's old and rusty and it's one of the longest five minutes of my life but I manage to break it and place the lock down by the fence. All I need to do now is push it and see if I can shift the rock behind it.

The electric current runs up the side and over the top of the gate so that if the gate is opened, it still continues around. What I do think is that I'll have to be quick. I can't be sitting forcing this gate for a long time. I look around me in what's essentially mainly moor but do a quick scavenge to find a long stick from a long-dead tree. It's not ideal and could be longer but it will

CHAPTER ELEVEN

allow me to put my arm through, get the stick underneath the rock and try to shift it.

Approaching the gate, I bend down and carefully place the stick through the wire and at the rock. I try to shift it with my arm alone and the rock lifts slightly but doesn't move fully. I'm going to have to give it one almighty go and that's going to involve me standing up to try and get as much power into that stick and deflect the rock out of the way. It's a bit of a gamble and I think about the fact that I'm going have to run off onto a moor. If people come out, will they then start to search and find a car at the end of the drive because it would take me a while to get back there? Do they have infrared scan around?

I'm unsure. I could wait; I could bring back hands on another day. I hunker down and look around me trying to check out what equipment is on the fences. I think to myself, *Sometimes, Paddy, you need to relax; you know where she is now.* I replace the lock, another feat of ingenuity holding it in my mouth and then trying to slam it back in. It will probably be best to have an expert come along and take a look at the systems lest my rashness gets me into trouble.

The rain begins as I make my way back to the car, which is annoying. Rain makes it easier to break in anywhere, gives me that extra sound and covers up my movements. As I reach the car and get in, I phone Hans Webber.

Hans is an old friend I've worked with before and will do many times more. I pulled his life around, having caught him doing lots of very, very nasty things but one thing that Hans is, is an expert on all electronics and communication systems—and with Hans on board, it will be easier to break in.

On return to the hotel, I get some sleep before briefly meeting up with Susan who explains the rather drab goings-on with the boys from the boat. I tell her to keep a wider breadth with them because once again they've spotted her and come over to say hello. She says she thinks the oldest one's just sweet on her and she might be right but she doesn't want to give the impression she's hanging around. Not just simply because she doesn't want them to know she's watching them but also because if he is sweet on her, he might actually make a pass or want to take things further. That's too much of an entanglement; it can get us involved before we want to be involved.

Around about teatime, Hans arrives, reaching our hotel in a taxi. I see him as I'm having dinner, but he doesn't acknowledge me and it's an hour later when I'm back in my room, that he knocks the door. I call Susan through and introduce the pair. Susan's here only to learn and there's no way she's coming out tonight but Hans has got a pleasant demeanour with him and after I've briefed him and we've talked through what we're going to do, he spends a little time explaining some of the gadgets to Susan. She sits in wide-eyed excitement. We both catch a little sleep before we head out that night, and now it's two a.m. and we're sitting at the end of the road. Hans has me wired-up with a camera so he can see what I see and he's sitting in the car ready to make a getaway if we need to. I complete a check of all my systems and then I head off onto the moor, walking up the track that leads to the house.

The house is essentially dark and I notice a guard at the gate, once again, hiding. I listen to all of their movements and Hans has me identify some feeds from the camera run and then he explains to me that I need to drop a certain box around a certain wire and then stay still. It takes him a moment before he tells me that I can climb the gate. It's a moment of trust when I simply climb up and fling myself over because if he's got it

CHAPTER ELEVEN

wrong, I'm going to be shaking like anything and the guard is going to come running. Once I'm over, I hear the hum of the electric fence continue.

Hans says he has the feed to the camera system and tells me to walk forward up to the house and just advise him which door I'm going in. I take a trip around to the rear and find there's three doors there, one of which seems to enter a garage. I find it open which means there must be people about patrolling and not just on the gate. Stepping into the garage, the lights flick on and I duck behind an expensive car. I hear the footsteps of someone come in, then I hear them go out and the light is switched off again. It won't be long before they're back on their round so I run over to the only door out and listen carefully. There's no sound so I open the door gingerly, taking out a small mirror and passing it through to see two empty hallways. Retracting the mirror, I move through the door quickly.

Hans says there's someone to my right-hand side as he must recognize the camera feed, so I move to the left. I head down the empty corridor. He's telling me in my ear that the upstairs' camera feeds seem to have no one, only the downstairs. As I pass a set of stairs, I quickly move up them walking on the outsides so as not to cause a creek. It takes time to develop a soft foot and previously being caught means that I've developed it very, very quickly because I didn't want to be caught a second time. The beating I got then taught me that.

The upper floor's in darkness and I put on a pair of infrared goggles which allow me to see quite clearly. There's a large room at the end of the hallway with a door that's open. Carefully, I move along and I can hear people sleeping. I step through, poke my head round the door and see a large bed with two women lying on it. The sheets are thrown back and

I recognize one as the model Doolan's been shooting. The other's a blonde-haired woman whom I haven't seen before. This is the master bedroom as far as I can tell and the blonde-haired woman has her arms around the Asian girl. As I said before, I try not to prejudge anything, so I simply make a note and step out.

Stepping back down that hallway, I see an open plan area. I move into it. There's a sofa, TV, everything in all the latest styles and on a coffee table in the middle, there's a large amount of white powder. There's a private kitchen area upstairs, as well as another bedroom and an office. There's a computer inside and I get a word in my ear to put a dongle into it, so I place one in the side of the computer leaving it for Hans to do his work.

I make my way back to the bedroom and quickly check through the wardrobe that's there but all I can see are women's clothes. A brief search through the dresser shows me a couple of guns. Small handguns, but all highly effective. As Hans is still working, I make my way through to the other bedroom.

I find it to be filled with pictures on the wall, pictures that I recognize. It must be very disconcerting to walk into somewhere and to see yourself so brazenly portrayed on every wall. There's something seriously wrong here but as I step through the entire top floor, I get no impression there's a man about or someone else here for these women. It all points to the white woman being the person in charge.

There's a call in my ear. Hans tells me to get the dongle and get out. I don't wait for an explanation. Somebody must have realised I'm here. Somebody understands that someone else is in the house and so with great haste, I make my way back to the office, grab the dongle and turn to run down the stairs. An

CHAPTER ELEVEN

alarm erupts in the house but I've hit the stairs before anyone on the top floor can react. I sprint down to meet a man turning around the corner to come up the stairs. I don't have time to lash out, I just drop my shoulder and clatter hard into him, driving him back into the wall on the other side of the hall.

He tumbles to the ground. I can hear footsteps coming behind me as I run for the garage door but as I reach it, someone appears from the hallway. I run the opposite direction but I don't have time as they slam into me and I hit the wall. There's good fortune though because the person that was following me in the hall without my knowing has raised the gun. As I hear the shot go off, the person who's tackled me gets hit in the shoulder. The wall holds me up and I push the man that tackled me backwards. My hand flies to the handle of the door, flinging it open.

I hear another shot as I step inside the garage. I think it hit the frame of the door behind me but I don't check, running for my life. I don't switch the garage light on, simply sprinting around the car that's there, down low, opening the other door. I hit the fence that's nearest to that backdoor as quick as I can, trusting that Hans would have switched it off. I throw myself over and run off into the dark hearing shots fired after me. I guess someone tried to follow me over the fence because Hans has reactivated it and I hear a cry in the dark.

I don't look back, but just keep running off into the moorland. Hans by now will be driving elsewhere and may not even come back for me, knowing I've headed off into the distance. Twenty minutes later, my lungs feel like there's no air left in them. My legs are sore as I've pumped as hard as I can to get away, so I sit down when I realize there's no pursuit.

My infrared goggles allow me to see what's behind, and

there's nobody coming. I then begin the weary trudge back across the island, walking the several miles back to Dervaig and to the hotel. Hans comes down to let me in when I give him a ring from outside the hotel and we head up to my room for a discussion. Hans checks I've got the dongle and I do. He says he thinks he wasn't detected fully only that they knew somebody was breaking into their systems.

I try to sleep that night but I keep hearing the gunshots and see the man who was in front of me, his shoulder shot through. Tonight was too close. I'll try doing things at much more of a distance tomorrow.

Chapter Twelve

The following morning, I take Hans and Susan out for a spot of breakfast in Tobermory. We discuss our next moves and I explain that Hans needs to go and pick up some surveillance from that house rather than anyone go back in again. 'I'll try and keep an eye on Mr. Doolan,' I say, 'so you can go to the house, see if you can get on to the phone lines or anything of the mobile connections, just get me anything to go on.'

'Am I stuck with the boys in the fishing boat again?' says Susan.

I nod my head. 'Absolutely, it hasn't come up with anything yet, but they will move. We know they've got something stored on Gometra. I'm thinking that might be their place for the stash until they can sell it and I'm wondering how much they know. Are they able to sell it? So far, we have a woman who runs another woman off for photographs with Mr. Doolan. We have a lot of boys on a boat who are burying something in the middle of the night, basically drugs, but we have no way of knowing where they're getting them from.

'We don't have all of the pieces at the moment and we must get them, which is why Hans needs to do surveillance as I reckon that woman is a drug dealer. She's got all the hallmarks of it, the surveillance systems, the guards around the property. How many other places up here have guards? Next to none and guards in the quiet, not on the door properly. They weren't that easy to spot. I'd also say the house is maybe four or five years old, very new-built, small but modern. Maybe somebody trying out a new line, muscling in on the area, and they certainly packed weapons.'

'Wouldn't the gunshots have alerted police or somebody last night?'

'No, Susan,' I say, 'people out here, hunting, shooting this, shooting that, you can explain it away far too easily.'

We head off on our separate ways, Susan's staying on the bay at Tobermory because the boat's still there. Hans sets off to do some undercover work and pick out more communications and I drive back to watch the Doolan house. I'm on a walk around and I realize that the equipment in the copse has all been taken back inside. There's obviously a special shoot set up for when Annie Doolan wasn't about. Doolan himself stays in all morning and through my binoculars, I can see him up in his office. Otherwise, there isn't much about. At one o'clock he heads out and I follow him in the car back to Tobermory. He's in a pub and sits down to a quiet lunch while I— sporting my extra arm—watch him from across the bar. As I'm sitting there, I'm joined by a woman and I recognize the blonde hair and the scar on the side of the face. 'Good afternoon, Miss Hunstanton,' I say. 'What brings you to this fine establishment today?'

'You always want to talk business when we both know it's a business I can't talk about.'

I laugh. 'I have a feeling you might be watching someone,' I say, and she looks a little shocked. 'Mr. Doolan,' I say with a

CHAPTER TWELVE

quiet voice, 'seems to be a remarkably interesting man for a lot of people.' She breaks out in a slight smile and then narrows her eyes wondering who I'm working for. I don't let her know and I don't do her the disservice of telling her who she's working for.

'He doesn't normally lunch,' she says. 'My guess is he's waiting for someone or something.'

'I agree with you, Miss Hunstanton and I think we should sit here and have a good conversation, make it look like we're here for some lunch ourselves.'

'Agreed,' she says, turns round, and calls over the barman. Ten minutes later, we're eating sandwiches and sitting on the far side of the pub from Jack Doolan. We're both sitting sideways so we can cast glances and no one has to look over their shoulder, but he seems to be reasonably carefree, tucking away into a pie with chips.

It's about half an hour later and after a lot of small talk that I really didn't want to get into, that someone of interest walks into the bar. It's the Asian woman and she's dressed in high boots, a short skirt and a tight blouse.

Sarah casts a glance over her shoulder and then looks at me. 'Bit classy for in here,' she says; 'very classy, although I hear she takes photographs.' Sarah looks at me.

'Let's cut the pretence,' I say. 'We both saw it—we both know what she's here to do.'

Sarah seems slightly shocked, but she holds her poise as the woman walks in, delivers about three words to Jack Doolan and then walks out of the bar. Jack Doolan packs up in a hurry and rushes out after her and Sarah tries to stand up quickly.

I put a hand on one of hers saying, 'Don't! You don't want to be too keen out that door; you don't know why he's in here, why she's been sent in. I haven't seen them meet like this before.' But Sarah ignores me, grabbing her stuff and running out the door, keen not to lose her prey. I stand up, throw some cash across to the barman and leave. I try to saunter out the door and not in any particular direction, taking in the whole **vista** of Tobermory. I don't see them but I see Sarah hurrying off down the street, seeking her car. I walk quickly behind her and as she gets into the driver's seat, I open the passenger side and step in. She looks at me with horrified eyes.

'No point in the both of us driving, is there?' I say. With gritted teeth, she drives off, **pulling** in behind a large black car. I tell her to pull back a bit but she tells me to mind my own business, it's her car, and she's doing the tail. I'm getting a little bit edgy about this now because she's too close, too easy to spot. And if this is them trying to mark us, it's too easy. I've wondered before about her experience in this game and I don't think it's a lot.

The black car continues driving out of Tobermory and down the east side of the Isle of Mull until eventually pulling off into a forest. The car rolls up in a car park and Sarah, despite my protestations, insists on following them into the car park and driving up to the far end. I see the Asian woman get out followed by Jack Doolan and then a large man. He starts walking around the car park looking at the cars in it, which is not difficult as there are only three. I grab hold of Sarah telling her to kiss me and not to stop. She's nervous now because she knows the large man is coming over to the car, but she does as asked and at the corner of my eye, I see him looking in at us. He stands there, openly watching us kiss before disappearing back to the car. I tell Sarah to keep kissing and as I watch beyond, I see Doolan and the Asian girl being told to get back in. The

CHAPTER TWELVE

car drives off and Sarah goes to follow it.

'Stop,' I say, 'we've just been marked.' She looks at me. 'What do you mean been marked? I wasn't followed.'

'No,' I say, 'but they know somebody's on to them. That's why they got Doolan here. They wanted to check if he's being followed and we were so close to him, there is no way they can't have marked us.'

'But they just left,' she says. 'It worked, kissing you worked. They think we're some sort of couple—even at the bar we looked like a couple.'

'Don't count your chickens,' I say. 'In the days that come, be incredibly careful. Stay somewhere public; don't go out in the dark.'

'You don't have to tell me my business,' she says. 'I do know how to tail people.'

'I'm sure you do,' I say, 'but just be aware. These people that Doolan's involved with, they're not nice.'

'What makes you say that? Tell me what you know,' she said.

I shake my head. 'I get paid to find this stuff out. I'm just giving you a friendly warning, one investigator to another, be incredibly careful.' She tuts at me, starts the car up and we drive back into Tobermory where I pick up my own car. As I'm about to drive off, there's a rap on the window and she's there again. I roll it down and she leans in quite provocatively. 'I don't suppose you want to drink later on. I could do with company to be frank,' she says.

'I think I mentioned before that I'm taken and if I was you, I'd drop your investigation and leave before they come after you.' I give those deadly serious eyes I've got, trying to make the point that I'm not messing about, not simply trying to chase her off my case and what I'm doing but she's quite determined and I don't think she's going to take the hint.

'You watch your own back, Paddy. I'm perfectly capable of looking after mine.' With that, she turns and struts away. She's certainly got the walk but I don't know how much experience she's got of handling these sorts of people. I've half a mind to just send Susan back to the office but with so many targets at the moment, I need help from her watching them and besides, she hasn't been marked yet. I come back to Dervaig that night where Hans has a report for me. He managed to tap into some phone conversations; he didn't get a lot, but what he did get was mention of graveyards, mention of bodies being disturbed. 'Our graves,' they said, 'our graves are in trouble.'

Chapter Thirteen

The next day begins with an early breakfast at five o'clock. I've decided that Susan shouldn't be out on her own with the current situation, something which she protests about, but when she sees the look in my eye, she backs down, knowing that she can't get out of it. We don't see Hans at breakfast as he's disappeared trying to dig up more about our mysterious woman in the house but we have a new lead now—about graves. It makes me think of Gometra but, unfortunately having been there, a grave was not being used as storage. It may have been graveyards in the past; it may have been a burial site, but there was nothing marked in the area that we found. A quick check of the local area tells me there are graveyards at Calgary Bay, and that coupled with the number of photographs of Calgary Bay taken by Keir, makes me decide we should stake it out.

We're fortunate it's a crisp day allowing Susan and myself to take the car down, park up, and sit on the beach for a while, binoculars out—cameras too—apparently appreciating the wildlife around us. I spend most of the day walking up and down with her, taking drinks of coffee out of a flask but there's not that many people about. Certainly, no characters we know.

When we drop by Jack Doolan's house, I realize that Annie

Doolan has returned from London, the expensive car sitting in the drive. From previous practice, he doesn't seem to do much while she's around and I can understand that. Too easy to get caught but also having the disturbance that day at the house when I nearly got shot, I wonder if the Asian woman's not going to be allowed out for a while.

Susan's becoming a little blasé about what we're doing here but then again, she wasn't shot at. I have eyes everywhere just in case someone comes and especially as I take a walk to the marked graves and cross the road that runs alongside Calgary Bay. There are a number of headstones, a little motif about what they are but as I look at the ground, I can't see any signs that it's been disturbed. And I mean any signs—even had it been carefully done, there still would be signs, though you'd have to look for them most closely. But there are none and it makes me wonder if I'm in the right place. It is a hunch and I am waiting for more from Hans.

Close to dinnertime, we take the car and run past the house where the boys from the boat live. We can see figures moving about but there's no real activity, nothing untoward, so we decide to head back to the hotel for some dinner.

Over dinner, I explain to her that I'll be going out that night and staking out the graves around Calgary Bay to see if there's any movement. She looks excited. 'A night out, Paddy,' she says, 'finally a night out; this could be fun.'

I shake my head. 'There's no way in this current climate you're coming out,' I say; 'no way at all. Once we finish here, you stay in your room and you've got my number and Hans' number if anything happens.'

'That's not fair,' she says. 'You're meant to be teaching me how to do this.'

CHAPTER THIRTEEN

'I am teaching you,' I say, 'but sometimes I can't put you in a position of risk when that risk is too great and you don't have the ability to deal with it.' This seems to hurt her.

'Is this cause you're dating my mom? Is this so you don't hurt her feelings?'

'She's made it clear to me, and it is the truth, that you and I have a professional relationship and I should do whatever I would do with anyone else in that relationship and not worry about her thoughts or feelings. That's not easy but that's what I'm doing and, therefore, you are staying in tonight.'

She's a bit stroppy about it and in a huff but after last time's fiasco, where she ended up getting caught and I had to rescue her, she gives me a promise that she's not going to cause any trouble and I do believe her. After all, last time, she was lucky to come out alive.

The night air is cool as I step out of the car, parked a little way down from Calgary Bay. I'm dressed up in black and I make my way along the fields close to the roadside before crossing it and stepping onto the grass beside the beach. The moon's out tonight and this gives an easy light to see by but also makes it darn cold. One of the downsides about surveillance is having to stay in the one place when all you want to do is get up and stretch your legs, remove the chill from your bones by a little bit of exercise. I have a flask of tea with me and a couple of provisions. I mean, it's just one of those long nights where you have to sit and do nothing, waiting for something else to happen.

Of course, it's never silent but the Bay does take on an eerie quality as the moonlight shines down off the water, causing a silvery reflection. I can hear birds in the night and the occasional thing scurrying. The odd car drifts by on the road but other than that, it's just Mother Nature going through her Twilight hours. It's three in the morning, I'm at a point of looking to give up, and that's when I spot him.

He's been on the far side of the Bay, just across the road but he hasn't been looking into the Bay and I think he's been looking towards the graves. I take my binoculars and look closer. The angle's acute and there's a possibility he's looking at the graves but there's also a possibility that he's looking to a patch of land to the south of them, a patch of land that doesn't seem to have any markings on it.

I remain where I am, not wishing to move to get closer lest he see me, and I spend the next hour watching him. Then abruptly, around about four a.m., he gets up and leaves. The sun won't be up until seven or eight and it seems strange to me that his vigil is cut short. He seems to shake as if cold and then lets out an almighty sneeze. It's not very professional but I reckon he's concluded that no one's about which, until I saw him, I was of the same opinion. I train my binoculars on him and watch the man disappear down the road and out of sight.

Several minutes later a car comes back heading towards Dervaig or maybe Tobermory and beyond. I'm beginning to think I should wrap it up myself and go home when I hear the distant putt of a motor and look out into the bay. It's a small tender and thankfully the water in the bay is calm as it heads in to stop on the beach. There are two figures on board, one seems quite tall and then a shorter figure gets out carrying a spade. He doesn't look around but instead runs over to the road, crosses it, and heads over to a patch of ground south of the graves.

I train my binoculars on the man that remains with the tender. He's got a black beard and, in the moonlight, I think

CHAPTER THIRTEEN

he's John from the *Sandra Jane* crew. The other chap's smaller and I can't quite catch the face but if it were Digsy, it wouldn't be out of place. The height seems about right as well as the stature, smaller, not as well-built. I swing my binoculars onto him, watching him dig. It's carefully done. The soil rolled back, not hacked up.

I see him pocket something and then roll the grass back over and spend some time fixing it up. It dawns on me that this must be what's happening—these smugglers are bringing in their drugs and leaving them here and somehow the crew of the *Sandra Jane* have heard of it and are now stealing them. Maybe they haven't put it out on the market yet and that's why they have the stash in Gometra. But why then did Keir end up dead? Could it be a word from the smugglers? But if so, just what's happened?

Everything sounds like a new development. We have the pictures of Keir with the Asian woman and that makes me think there could be a line there? Was he having an affair and got caught? Did this woman in the fortified house find out and decide to take him out? Was he touching graves he wasn't meant to? And did the boys from the boat have a disagreement with him? Did he find out what they were doing? And was he not actually in on the action or was he in and made a mistake so they disposed of him? But why on Gometra? Why leave him there? It's all supposition at the moment and I need to find out more.

As these thoughts go through my head, I see a car return and stop across from the graves. Fair play to Digsy, he's quick, and he's disappeared off into the darkness as the car sits, looking out. The tender has been moved along the beach to the far side where the moonlight isn't shining and John has himself well secluded. I see the light go on in the car and a man stuffing himself. I don't think it's burger and chips, but it's something, although I don't know where he's got it at this time of night unless he returned to cook it himself.

He sits there for an hour, polishing off whatever he brought with him before the car turns and drives away again. At this point, Digsy races back to the graves, does a quick bit more tidying up and then runs back across the road and to the tender. As he's about to get in, he shows something to John who nods, his hand on Digsy's head and then pushes the tender back out into the water. They both jump in; I assume they're heading back out of the bay.

I sit and wait, watching the tender disappear, no doubt the *Sandra Jane* is out of the bay around the corner and I'm annoyed that we didn't have someone trailing the voice on the boat but after the gunfire, it was right to keep Susan with me. Once the tender is out of sight, I make my way across the road, step past the marked graves and find the area of land that was disturbed. Looking down, I can see fine lines, the grass has been brushed over them but having a close inspection I can see where to pull the turf up.

As I am about to dig it up, I see the headlights of a car coming in the distance, so I disappear off along the roadside into a hedge where I'm still able to see the graves. The car stops across from them, a man gets out and walks over with a flashlight. It's the same guy who's been here before but he looks much more urgent as if somebody's had a word with him. As he kneels down in front of one of the graves, I see he's got a small spade in his hand and he's digging it up, rolling back the grass. Then I hear him say one word, 'Bollocks!'

He stands up, looking around in a frenzy as if he whoever

CHAPTER THIRTEEN

has done this would be standing looking at him going, 'hahaha'. But he doesn't clock me. I'm well enough hidden and I don't move. I see him get his mobile and he continues to stand there, looking down at the ground. He seems edgy, annoyed, and then he gets more so as another car comes along the road. It's black, seems similar to the one that dropped the Asian woman off in front of Jack Doolan's.

Two men get out of the front of the car, one going to the rear and opening it. I see a woman step out, she's tall, about six feet tall and built strongly. Her hair is cut short and as the moonlight splashes across her face, I have to say she looks a fearsome creature. The face is set tight, angry looking, and I watch her walk up to the graves where the first man seems to be shaking. The woman looks down into the grave and the back of her hand swings, catching the man across the jaw. It's quite a strike and I can hear the contact from where I am. The woman turns around almost in a huff, and then pulls out a gun and turns and puts it on the forehead of the man who apparently was meant to be protecting the graves.

He starts to shake and I see him go down to his knees, begging with her, pleading with her for his life. He starts to wet himself. I wonder if he's seen her do this before. That's the trouble with drug running, there's no messing about, there's no second chances, there's just straight in and well, you know. But I also note that the gun doesn't have a silencer on it and she's by a roadside and would have to pick up the body and take it somewhere else. When it's one of your henchmen, you don't tend to just leave a body lying around, especially if it's beside the site of your drug stash, so I doubt she is going to kill him right now. However, if I were in his position, I'd probably want a lot more clarification on that.

She withdraws the gun and he stands up, thanking her as she turns her back but then she turns around and delivers a kick right between the legs, which causes him to crumble to the ground, holding on to whatever's left of his family planning. She then puts another kick up straight to the head and he falls to the ground. She struts back to the car and the other two men get back in the front and they drive off. The surveillance man is still lying on the ground, clutching at himself but gradually he gets to his feet and hobbles his way back to the car, turns around, and then drives off towards Dervaig, and possibly the large house beyond where his mistress lives.

Personally, if I were him, I'd have driven the car the other direction and kept going and never stopped until I was in a different country. But then I've never been a henchman so maybe there's other things that tie you to them or there are things that make you want to stay. It certainly wasn't the looks of the woman because unlike the Asian woman, she is quite manly and strong, not something you would see in a magazine. Not that I'm saying there's anything wrong with looking like that, it's just making me think that it's some other sort of power that has got this surveillance man beholden to her.

I wait in my hidey hole for half an hour after everyone's disappeared, scanning the area around me in case they have another party waiting, another party identifying anyone that goes near the graves. When I can see no one, I make my way, find my car hidden at the roadside, jump in, and drive back to the hotel. It's six in the morning and I crash in my bed, knowing it's only going to be a couple of hours sleep. As I haven't contacted her, Susan will still be waiting in her room. I hope she hears the door closing because I'm not getting back up to tell her.

Chapter Fourteen

I stir by nine o'clock when there's a knock at the door. Getting up, I put on my dressing gown, open the door to find a fully dressed Susan ready for the day.

'I haven't had breakfast yet,' she says. 'I was just wondering if you wanted to come down for it or not. You look like rubbish.'

'Well, thank you,' I say, 'not all of us have had a bed for the night.'

'Well, that was your choice. I would have been out there with you.' She gives me that smug satisfied look that any teenager does when they've won an argument with you and yes, she is right, but she didn't have to rub my nose in it. I wonder if I weren't dating her mom, would she treat her employer this way?

But I say I'll be down very shortly and turn, close the door, and find my shower. The water doesn't do a lot to revive me. I still feel quite bleary eyed when I join Susan for breakfast. I manage to get some bacon, eggs, beans, and some toast which at least stops my stomach groaning even if it doesn't bring me back to a level of full awareness.

Susan still seems excited, asking where we're going today. I wonder if she realizes I've been out all night and I might not want to go too far. But she is correct, and we do need to look at what's going on. I tell her about the graves and about what's happened, but it also makes me wary and I tell her that. If they know things are being disturbed, these people might start coming after anyone that they see around and for this reason, she's certainly not leaving my side.

She also seems extremely disappointed when I tell her that this is her last day up in Mull as she's getting the ferry this afternoon. Things are just getting too hot and I need to make sure that she's safe and so it's with a huff that we return to our rooms and plan out the morning. I decide we should go and look where the crew of the *Sandra Jane* have got to although they'll probably be in their beds. We'll also see if there's any activity around them and if they are known to be smugglers. I'm still struggling to piece together what happened to Keir. Did he just get caught on the wrong side of a love triangle? Did Jack Doolan invite him along to the shoot at some point when he shouldn't have, meaning the boy was silenced, put away? If that's the case, Doolan was very matter of fact about it but I also saw photographs that were taken from a distance of the boy photographing the woman and that makes me think it was done surreptitiously.

Had Doolan wandered upon the boy doing this? Did he tip off the smugglers or has that nothing to do with it? Keir was working on the boat, the *Sandra Jane*, and they were nicking drugs from people they shouldn't have. Did Keir get caught one night? Did Keir decide he was taking things in to the authorities and the crew of the *Sandra Jane* disposed of him? It would make sense taking a boat round to Gometra to do that but why display him? Why not just simply throw him over the side and say he didn't turn up for work? Things just seemed a bit weird, especially leaving a naked body. What was the point

CHAPTER FOURTEEN

in that?

When Susan's packed, I tell her to leave the bag in the hotel room and we'll come back for it. Her hair is out of her long ponytail, splaying across the back of the black jacket she's wearing and with her jeans and boots on, she's ready for a bus trip back to Stranraer where no doubt her mother will greet her, delighted she's out of the firing line but at the same time having to deal with a stroppy daughter. Susan walks out ahead of me at the front door of the hotel and it's as she's stepping through, I clock the car opposite, long and black. 'Susan!' I shout.

I see a hand grab her as she's whisked out of my view. As I step through the door to try and retrieve her, I take a punch to the face that comes like a sledgehammer. It drops me to the ground and somebody reaches over me, but I swing my leg up and catch him with a boot to the face. My head is still ringing but I'm forcing myself to concentrate and see a man dragging Susan across to the black car, throwing her into the back.

I manage to struggle to my feet and sway to the left to avoid a punch from the man who attacked me. I drive a knee up into his stomach and he crumples down to receive an elbow from me into the back of his neck. The other man's back over, having thrown Susan in the car, and makes a grab for me but he seems to be unsure of himself. I think he went for my left arm, except I don't have one and having realized that, he didn't seem to know what to do. For his ineptitude and inaccuracy, he receives a kick to his knee that causes him to bend down and receive a knee to the face.

As I turn back for the first attacker, the car window opposite rolls down and I see Susan's face with a gun at the side of it. I raise a single hand in defeat and receive a punch for my troubles right to the gut that causes me to double up. I'm then picked up and thrown into the backseat as well. The doors lock and I look across to see the man from last night who was keeping an eye on the graves.

I stay quiet, trying not to look at him as though I've seen him before. He's still holding the gun to Susan's head and so I sit back as the car drives off. The journey's not long and looking out of the window, I know where we're going. We take a turn into that long drive up to the fortified house, up to the gates at the front with a guard hidden out of the way.

As I'm told to step out of the car, I hear the electric hum of the fence and look around. I'm hoping Hans is keeping surveillance on the place but I don't know, he might just be doing his electronic side, listening to the phones if he couldn't get a good camera up. I pray I'm wrong as once again I'm punched in the face and then dragged into the house, Susan behind me.

We're taken in via the front door round through a corridor with pictures on the walls, neat and ornate, and then through a door I don't recognize. It leads into a basement which is cold and damp and not had much work on it. It looks like a wet room, easy to clean down and that scares me. I'm dragged through and then my hand is handcuffed before being taken above my head where the cuff is tied to a device in the ceiling. It sounds like some sort of mechanical mechanism, making me wonder what it's for but I don't have long to wait to find out. The handcuff starts to ascend and my feet with it until they hang just off the ground. If I stretch with my tiptoes, I'm able to make contact, able to take some of the weight off my wrist, but it's awkward to do. I'm ending up between taking the strain of the weight on my feet or taking the strain of a

CHAPTER FOURTEEN

hand-cuffed hand. I'm not sure it's working correctly because I have only the one arm, but it feels like everything's ripping through my shoulder.

The guys laugh. I receive a couple of punches to the stomach, which makes Susan scream. There's a second device and her hands are cuffed, and she's put on it. However, they don't raise her up the way they did to me. Instead, the three men walk around her and I see hands going where they shouldn't. She's starting to cry, starting to twist away from them as rough hands go to places she doesn't want them. I spit over on one of them and receive another punch to the stomach.

As the guys crowd around her, a voice comes into the room that causes them to scatter to the sides of it. Wearing a long black dress, leather boots coming out underneath, and a smart waistcoat, I see the woman who stepped out of the car last night. I also recognize her as the woman who was lying beside the Asian in the bed when I snuck in here. She makes her way down the concrete steps that we went down so recently and walks over to Susan who is snivelling, putting a hand across her chin and then surveying her. She nods as if satisfied, and then steps to me.

'Patrick Smythe,' she says, and the voice is a hoarse, croaky sound like she smoked too many cigarettes in her life. 'Or do we just call you Paddy? That's what everyone else calls you. Bit of a name for yourself. I want to know what you're doing here, Mr. Smythe.'

'I'm here with my friend taking photographs of the wildlife, just out and about.' The woman nods to a man on the side and steps back away from me. He delivers three hard punches to my stomach then another one to my head. I'm sore, I'm beat up, but I'm not feeling that weak yet. Stretching my good arm, I reach with my hand, grabbing the mechanism that comes from the roof, this allows me to get a bit of traction and I swing a leg around catching the man in the face sending him reeling backwards. The woman nods to another man who comes over and holds me while the first man gets back up and delivers four more punches to my chin. I can taste the blood in my mouth but I keep my eyes staring at him letting him know I'm coming for him.

The woman walks back in front of me. 'And so when, Mr. Smythe, did you take up wildlife photography? I know who you are—I just don't know why you're here. Who is it you're investigating?'

This makes it awkward. How do I play this? 'That's usually an investigator, client privilege,' I say. But the woman walks up to me, puts her hand under my chin and says, 'That's not the tone we like, Mr. Smythe. Some cooperation would be better.' And with that she turns around to the thugs behind me and tells them to come forward. My shirt's torn off me and my trousers are taken down and I'm left in just my pants. A few more blows are beaten into me before the woman steps back in front and traces a line across my chest with her finger.

'Better cooperation please, Mr. Smythe.' I spit in her face and she takes her hand up, wiping it off. 'I see persuading you doesn't work. Let's see how you react to your friend getting some of the same treatment.' I see the men walk forward, happily, leering, and Susan's handcuffs are taken off briefly but only so they can remove her jacket, her top, and her jeans before she's left hanging in just underwear. The woman comes back in front of me.

'Quite frankly, I'm happy to go all the way with this and leave you both hanging with nothing on,' she says, 'but that would

CHAPTER FOURTEEN

be unfriendly to guests. Now tell me what you're doing, Mr. Smythe.'

My mind races to think of a good cover story. I've been around Jack Doolan and we've been around the boat. I'm thinking she doesn't know about the boat, the *Sandra Jane* and its crew and so I tell her. 'Annie Doolan. She wants to know what her husband gets up to, she wants to know why he's got a locked basement, and she has me investigating him, finding out what he's doing.'

'And what is he doing?' asked the woman.

'He's photographing an Asian woman, proper photographs, professional photographs,' I say. The woman turns her back to me, seems to be thinking before she issues a shout up the stairs. There's a sound of high heels coming down the concrete steps and I turn my head to see the Asian woman in a dressing gown. She makes her way across the floor before allowing herself to be wrapped up by the older, larger woman.

'He's doing that for me,' she says. 'When you have beauty like this, it's good to capture it, don't you think, Mr. Smythe?' I nod. 'And he's quite good with a camera,' she says, 'but I think I need to check out your story because someone else is saying the same thing.' There's another shout and a man brings down an older woman and I immediately recognize the blonde hair of Sarah Hunstanton, even though her scar's on the other side of her face from me.

'Miss Hunstanton here says that she's also been hired by Annie Doolan, looking to photograph her husband, find out what he's doing. I frankly don't care, Mr. Smythe, if he's being investigated and I don't care that you know he takes photographs for me, of my beloved, but I don't believe you, what you're telling me about your business. So, while I check out your story and find out if you're telling me the truth, you'll remain a guest. Miss Hunstanton will also join you. Unfortunately, this room only accommodates two people, so your young ward, Susan, I believe, will have to join me upstairs.'

This scares me because while they're down here, they might paw over her, they might even hit her but up there, who knows what they'll do? This woman could ply her on drugs and then just use her. When I look at the Asian woman wrapped up in the grasp of our captor, her eyes look cold, sullen as the man takes Susan down. They rudely kick her clothes to the side of the room and Susan is taken away by the Asian woman up the concrete steps. Sarah Hunstanton is then brought over and one of the men turns around and asks if she should be dressed or not.

As the older woman starts to go up the concrete steps to leave us, she turns back and says to me, 'What do you think, Mr. Smythe? Sometimes the boys are gonna have their fun.'

And with that she nods at the man who steps forward, stripping Miss Hunstanton down to her underwear before handcuffing and raising the mechanism, so she's in a similar predicament to myself, toes barely touching the ground, pain going through her wrists. The men start to step forward and paw all over before they are called away by their mistress leaving the two of us hanging there together. The woman's starting to weep but occasional pain brings her back to her senses.

'How the hell do we get out, Paddy? How do we get out of here?' she says and all I can think is Hans had better be watching.

Chapter Fifteen

I'm not quite sure how long I've been hanging here. At some point, I either passed out or fell asleep but the pain kept jolting me awake. I feel like my shoulder is going to separate and despite how often I've looked, I can't see how to get my hand out of the cuff. Beside me, Sarah Hunstanton is not doing well. Several times, she screamed out loud, thrashed about, which can only add to her pain. She's had moments of panic and I've tried to talk her down, but it's not been easy. I think she never banked on something like this. She probably reckons she was looking for simple missing husband or someone who was playing around and how she got into this, she's probably not sure. At least I knew murder was afoot when I came up here but my main concern at the moment is Susan.

I saw the woman's eyes looking at her and I see how she keeps the Asian woman which is giving me quite a fright. I certainly don't want her to end up on a beach with Jack Doolan, wafting his camera in her face. But the simple matter of the fact at the moment is I have only one real prayer and that's Hans. Back in his day he was a good criminal, he could operate in the dark easily, and was also not afraid to take chances. He's also grateful enough to me not to just walk off and leave me. I doubt Sarah Hunstanton has anyone watching her back and, given the company she was walking into, that was a mistake on her part.

I'm guessing it's the middle of the night though I'm not sure how long's passed. My deduction comes from the fact that the house is quiet, noticeably quiet, similar to when I broke in, but the silence could be due to the fact we're downstairs and can't hear that well. I didn't hear that much throughout the day though either although the pain in my arm didn't really help. The door to the cellar opens but quietly, with barely a sound. It shuts behind and there's soft footsteps on the concrete, not confident ones but cautious ones, taking a step at a time. I can imagine the figure starting to bend down to see into the room. Beside me, Sarah is awake and she turns her head and sees someone, she starts screaming. There's a burst of energy from the person, jumping off the stairs and racing over here. A hand claps across her mouth and a voice says 'quiet', with just a hint of a German accent.

'You're not looking too good, Paddy,' says Hans. 'Good job I came here. Can you tell this woman to be quiet?'

I'm not in my normal fettle but I turn to Sarah and with quiet tones urge her to shush. She looks at me, her eyes wide with fear but I tell her this is a friend and she'll be out of her cuffs in a minute. Once assured that Sarah is going to stay quiet, Hans starts to unpick the lock on her handcuffs, and then my own. He's much quicker at this than I and inside of thirty seconds, I'm standing, trying to bring my arm down. It feels strange after being hung up for so long and even when I do bring it down, it feels like it's still up there. We're both standing in our underwear and Hans hasn't had the foresight to bring a full change of clothing for myself and a woman he's never met, so

CHAPTER FIFTEEN

it looks we're escaping that way.

'Have you seen Susan?' I ask.

'She disappeared off in the car,' says Hans. 'I managed to get a tracer to it but we need to be quick to catch up.' I nod and indicate that he should lead the way. Sarah stands shaking, but I offer my hand, which she takes, and I lead her up the concrete steps behind Hans. He has switched off a lot of devices, cameras and such, but we still need to be extremely cautious.

Hans opens the door and stares out into the corridor. He looks left and right and then steps aside quietly, urging us on behind him. He shuts the door behind us and then leads us out towards the garage, the route I'd come in before. We move quickly inside with no lights on and reach the garage door. I don't know how often they checked us in the cellar, but they definitely did, so we may have little time. I look out and see the grass before the fence. I know we're going to have to run all the way over. But before we do, I tap Hans on the shoulder. 'Did you see where they put our stuff?' I say.

'From what I heard in the conversations,' he says, 'it got taken upstairs to where the boss is. I think it may still be up there. Do you want me to fetch it?' I tell him I think he's done enough, and as I've seen upstairs so I'll go. He stays with Sarah and can get her out if anything goes wrong.

She doesn't want me to leave but I tell her Hans is good and he'll take care of her and at the end of the day, he's the obvious option. He's got two arms, he's built like a brick outhouse and he's done a far better job of creeping around than we have. Moving back to the garage, I open the door to the hallway and see nothing there. I'm feeling a little bit groggy but I'd rather risk myself for my clothes than send Hans again. Making my way along the hall, I listen intently before finding the stairs that leads up, shutting the door behind me and climbing. I still keep an ear out in case anyone's patrolling because the boss is away, but I need not have worried; everything seems to be a lot quieter now she's not about. Walking through the lounge, I find my jeans and top scattered about, my wallet laid out on a table. Sarah's clothes are there too along with her items. They've obviously been rifled through.

I now need to make a call. If they know my name, and more still, if they have managed to get Susan's name from her, Maggie and her other daughter could be in jeopardy. But I can't do that at the moment, so I dress quickly back into my clothes before gathering up my personal items, securing them on me and then taking Sarah's in my arms.

It would be handy if there was some sort of plastic bag to carry the stuff in, but there isn't. So, I have to wrap my arm around them tight which makes me rather ungainly as I walk. Making my way downstairs, I listen at the door and hold my position as I hear footsteps walking past. I give them three minutes before I awkwardly open the door forcing my hand out from the bundle that is Sarah Hunstanton's clothes. I creep along the hallway into the garage to find Hans there. Sarah looks at me with relief and she begins to dress. In some ways, I think maybe we should run and she should do that later but it's going to be awkward carrying a bundle of clothes and in fairness, she's quick about it.

Two minutes later, Hans is outside the garage door looking around cautiously. He then leads us across the back lawn to a point in the fence. I can hear the hum but Hans grabs part of the fence, pushing one tip down and one of the wires out insisting we get through quickly. We do and then he steps through himself before turning back. I see him remove several

CHAPTER FIFTEEN

wires off the fence and realize that he's channelled the current to go round, leaving a safe space to get through. It's always much easier when you bring Hans in.

We disappear over the moor until I see my car. As we get inside and shut the door, Hans drives off. I turn round to Sarah Hunstanton, to see how she is, but the woman's in tears in the back seat. She may have had a tough life before, may have seen things in the force down South but it's quite something else to be held, captured, mistreated like she was and even now, she's in the company of two men she doesn't really know.

'They're going to know where you've been staying,' I say, 'you need to stay low for a couple of days until we can sort this out.'

'Sort it out? Take it to the police right now,' she says. 'I have contacts, don't worry. It'll be a properly done investigation—they'll move quick.'

I shake my head. 'We bring them in and Susan's dead. Hans has got a tracker on her; we need to go and get her. I can drop you off before we do that but you need to stay low, hidden out of the way or you can come with us.' I see Hans raise an eyebrow at this. 'But if you do, you'll be staying out of the way when we go for her.'

Sarah looks at me and I can see her trying to calculate what's really happening when she gives a nod and says she'll come with us. I think that's probably because she's so scared, she needs to find anyone she can trust.

Hans hands me one of his devices, it's got a screen with some buttons underneath it. And as he switches it on at the side, it starts to beep, there's a GPS map showing, and we see that something is on the move. I recognize the layout of the road and it's Jack Doolan's house. I feel a little bit of fear inside wondering what they're going to get Susan to do. But then the car moves off again, tumbling further away across Mull. Part of me wonders if they dropped her at Jack Doolan's but Annie was still about. I ask Hans how long I was held captive for and he says twenty-four hours. It certainly feels like that because I'm famished but I doubt Annie would have left to go back to London. And so, I tell him to tail the car, not to stop at Doolan's.

The car on the tracker eventually stops not far from where we took the ferry to Ulva. It's close to the water, down by a beach and we stop our car short of it. I tell Sarah to stay in the car, to keep it dark, no lights, and we'll be back. If we come back in a hurry, I want her in the driver's seat ready to go.

With Hans, I creep forward looking for something happening and it's not difficult to spot. Once you're off the road and down towards the shore, there's a set of lights and I can see Jack Doolan holding a camera. My heart sinks but when I look there, there's no one in shot. Instead, off to the side, I can see the Asian woman wrapped up in a gown but she seems to be shivering against the cold. Beside her is Susan still dressed in the clothes she was wearing when we were caught, but I get the feeling it's not for long.

I can see the older woman, the boss of this outfit and for once her expression seems to be replaced by something approximating to delight. She has a leer and she looks over towards the two women and I want to just rush in and grab Susan. But we can see several bodyguards standing around.

I whisper some words to Hans. He hands me a short club. One of the problems I have is I can't simply walk up behind somebody and take them out quickly and quietly with just one hand. When you've got two hands you can cover their mouth while you do whatever damage you need to. So instead I've got something to clock them hard across the back, and if you do it right, you can usually knock them out. Hans, however, has a weapon. It's silenced and he's keeping it close to him but we're going to try and do this in a stealthy fashion. We move out to the outer guards, two men standing some distance away and creep up behind them. I take one out with a large 'thunk' to the back of his head. He drops like a stone while the other is grabbed by Hans. I try not to kill anyone and Hans is under that instruction too as it just makes it more complicated later on with the police. But as his guard drops senseless to the ground, I move in closer and see another two bodyguards.

The boss is leering over at Susan but tells the Asian woman to move first. She steps forward and drops her gown off. I can see Susan tremble because she knows what's coming. But one of the bright sides to the Asian woman revealing herself is that the guards both turn around for a look and that's when they both fall to the ground. Hans then steps forward, pulling out his gun and then shows himself to everyone. 'Hold still, don't move. Susan, with me.' he says.

One thing about her is that Susan picks up on things quickly and she turns and runs to Hans. We start to walk backwards and I look behind me to see if there's any more guards, but I can't clock any. The boss steps forward telling Hans he's making a mistake, telling him to bring her property back. I'm sure that sends a chill through Susan because it sent one through me. Hans is watching her carefully as he steps backwards away but his foot catches something and he tumbles to the ground.

Within an instant the woman's firing and she's caught him somewhere in the leg. His gun falls to one side and the boss woman steps forward. I reach down and grab Hans' gun and fire quickly towards her. It's a rough shot but it has the desired effect as she runs for cover, along with the naked Asian woman and Jack Doolan. I then take a shot at his lights, the ones that light up umbrellas to make sure he gets a good picture of the women. With two shots, they tumble over, one blown out by bullet, the other crashing to the ground before smashing.

I reach down for Hans, who's groaning, and I swing my arm underneath him and drag him to his feet. Susan reaches down also and grabs his other arm. Together we run as hard as we can. I hear shots passing behind me but with her bodyguards gone, I'm not sure if she'll pursue. The boss is crying out for them but none are responding.

We reach the car and dump Hans unceremoniously into the rear, Susan getting in with him. I jump in the front and see Sarah Hunstanton's shocked face.

'I heard gunfire,' she said, 'what happened?'

'Never mind that,' I say. 'Go! Just go!' and we drive off into the Mull night.

About half an hour later, we pull into a car park that leads to a track into some forest. Strangely enough at this time of the morning, no one's there, and I'm able to look at Hans' wound. I patch it up as best as I can but he's going to need to see a doctor. Taking up my mobile, I phone two people. Firstly, a doctor I know, one from back home who happens to be an old flame. She lives on the west coast and she'll drive down, saying she'll meet us in Oban. She obviously understood the seriousness of my voice because she will be leaving her husband and kids to come down to do it.

The second call I make to my old friend, Martha. She's surprised to hear from me because she's had nothing else to feed me, information wise, about what's going on. I say to her, 'time to mobilize' and explain the situation. Martha is going to go down to Stranraer to get Maggie and Kirsten, Susan's sister, and keep an eye on them.

This has all taken a turn for the worse. With Hans shot, he's going to be out of action and I'm going to have to go dark now because the drug dealers will be looking for us. But I can't operate on my own here. I'm going to need someone else because there are a number of parties involved so it looks like Susan will have to become of age. I just hope she's up to it.

Chapter Sixteen

There's an early boat that I can use to get Hans off Mull. One of the things I'm worried about is just how many people this drug dealer has, who might simply turn up with a car, or if we'll be seen at the ferry. On the other hand, if we do catch the ferry, maybe they'll think we're leaving. Will they follow? I reckon they must be in a mess at the moment and I'm sure she's wondering what we're doing. I could do with my prosthetic as well, to make more of a disguise, but it's back in the hotel, so I decide to make a run for it.

Daylight's about to come round and the ferry leaves in an hour or two. So, I tell everyone to get in and we drive down to the ferry terminal, stopping on the way when I see a petrol station to buy some food. There's nothing nutritious but it's been twenty-four hours since Sarah and I ate. Susan, apparently, was fed a rather splendid meal and looked after rather well, if somewhat leered over, fawned at, and basically been told that she would be a pet for most of the rest of her life, possibly having to partake in activities of a bedroom nature which she certainly wouldn't have been up for.

In all this, Susan is sat with Hans as he has started to take on a fever. She's working with him, talking to him and telling him he's going to be okay. There's a steely-eyed resistance that I've

CHAPTER SIXTEEN

seen in her mother, the one that just says 'let's get the job done and get on with it' rather than faff about with worries about how she's feeling. I knew I picked well when I chose Susan to be my assistant. It's just I didn't really want to bring her into something like this as quickly as it has happened.

So today is going to pan out like this: we get Hans over to the other side to my friend and doctor, Lorraine, then we come back and sort out what's happening. I'll encourage Sarah Hunstanton to stay with Lorraine because I work better without someone like that around. I might have to verge on the side of the not-so-pure-and-white to get this done and as a former officer, she might not agree to that.

I stroll down to the ferry-booking office and manage to get us tickets. We have to wait approximately an hour while the ferry arrives before boarding. We're out in broad daylight and I can't see anyone clocking us. Once on the ferry, we set Hans in a corner upright with a blanket around his legs. He's not looking well and one of the staff asked how he is and I tell her, this is why we're taking him off, he's just got a fever and we're running into the hospital because the one on Mull can't deal with it. I got sympathy, which is a testament to the crew of the ferry, and she asked if she could bring anything for us. I thank her and say no, wishing to keep a low profile again.

Susan brings back food from the ferry's canteen and I hungrily eat. I'm not actually sure what's even in front of me—it's some sort of breakfast. And I say that not because it's unappealing or unappetizing, it's just that I eat it quickly because of my hunger that I barely stop to see what's going in my mouth. Sarah doesn't eat quite so quickly and I think things are beginning to sink in with her about how close she was to having something really nasty happen to her.

When we get on the other side, I say to Sarah, 'I'm going to get Hans into the capable skills of my friend Lorraine. She's a proper doctor but we have somewhere quiet for her to go to keep Hans. We don't use it much, but it's got all the gear and I think you should go with her, just keep out of the picture until I can get this resolved.'

The woman looks at me, nodding, but then turns and says, 'Do you need help, Paddy? I'll help you if you need it.'

'I'm guessing you haven't done this sort of thing a lot,' I say. 'I'm guessing you're hoping that your private investigator days were filled with cheating husbands, insurance scams, things like that. Things that while of themselves are not good, certainly wouldn't get you shot at, tortured, and held up.'

She smiles, 'No. I certainly didn't want this.'

'Then go and stay with Lorraine for a couple of days,' I say, 'I'll be done then, and this will be concluded in one way or another.'

She thanks me and turns back to her food, still picking away at it. The ferry runs quite smooth and when we arrive in Mull, I drive off and stop in a car park just out of the town. Across from me in one of those cars with a large boot, which looks more like a van, is Lorraine. She's got long, dark-brown hair which hangs exactly the way I remember it. Now she doesn't look the same as she did back in the day when I charmed her at the cinema, but she does still have that lovely smile that could warm me from anywhere. They say that sometimes in your heart, flames don't go out even when you move on to someone else and she's one of them. She's married now and she's got kids but if she asked me to run for something, I'd still run and in fairness, she's run here. Not that I'm looking to rekindle any old flames but it is good to see a face of a friend.

CHAPTER SIXTEEN

She steps across to me throwing her arms around me, 'Paddy, you only ever call when you're in trouble.' When we break off, I look at her and smile. She was the one that put that rule in, she was the one that said we shouldn't spend any time with each other outside of when I needed her. She was worried that I would mess up her family and in reality, she's probably right because as I look at her now, I'm not seeing a doctor. I'm seeing an old friend and a very dear lover.

'Let's get a look at him,' she says, and I take her to the rear of her car where she takes off Hans' bandages, rolls up his jeans and looks at the wound. 'Okay,' she says, 'get him in the car. He'll be all right. I'll get it out, we'll deal with it, but he'll be off his feet for a few days at least.'

'We'll cope. I've got a new partner,' I say and introduce Lorraine to Susan. As I help Hans into Lorraine's car with one of his arms around my neck and the other around Susan's, I can smell the perfume. It's the one I bought her almost fifteen years ago and she told me she'd never wear it unless she was meeting me. She's true to her word—that's one thing you can say about Lorraine.

Once we have Hans packed in the back of her car, Sarah beside him, I tell Susan to go back to our car and take a moment with Lorraine. There's a part of me could just leave all this, take her by the hand and disappear off together, never looking back. But that would be so wrong with the life she's built. And it's not that she's better than Maggie, it's just there's moments when you wish you could have everything, especially if you're fortunate enough to meet that many good people in your life.

'You've got someone, Paddy, haven't you?'

I nod. 'Is it that obvious?'

'It is to me. What's she like?' asked Lorraine.

'See the one behind me? Susan's mother—she's called Maggie and she's like that but with dark hair, a little bit older, and even more steel than that one.'

'Happy for you, Paddy.'

'How's Robert and the kids?' I ask.

'Wonderful as ever.' I see her looking at me up and down. 'Damn that bomb blast, Paddy,' she says and reaches forward, giving me a gentle kiss on the lips. I hope Susan is not watching because I kiss back.

'Take care of them,' I say before turning away and my head wallows in her words, *Damn that bomb blast.* When my arm was separated from me, so was Lorraine because she couldn't handle it and she couldn't handle me that time. I don't blame her, sometimes in life things are moving on and they're moving well, then all of a sudden, your tracks get ripped apart through no fault of your own. In a different life, her kids would be my kids. Still, there's a case to go and solve and I need to be on my game, not reminiscing on a life that never was.

I get back in my car and together with Susan, we drive to a car dealership to pick up a bit of an old banger for a couple of hundred quid. Leaving my car, we take the newly purchased vehicle back on the ferry, and arrive back in Mull later that afternoon. It's when we're on the boat that Susan asks me the question I hoped she wasn't going to.

'Bit more than a friend then, bit more than a medical acquaintance,' she says.

'Don't worry. Lorraine's an old, old friend back in the days when I had my other arm. You're not old enough to know you can love more than one person.'

'What happened then?' she asks.

I shake my head. It's not something I bring up in front of

people, it's not something I want people to know. So, I say to her, 'Sometimes love just isn't enough.' Thankfully, she takes the hint in that and doesn't ask any more.

Back on Mull, I drive back to our hotel and realize there's a car watching it. So, I make a phone call to the owner asking him to go and pack up everything in our room, place it in two suitcases, drive in his car and drop it off at a car park well out of Dervaig. He seems a little surprised but I tell him I'll pay him cash in hand when he gets there and so he agrees. True to his word, he arrives with no one tailing him and I hand over the money, thanking him for our stay.

'And if anyone asks,' I say, 'tell them we've left, gone away.' He nods, asking if we're in some sort of trouble. I nod and tell him to keep quiet and not get involved.

In order to close this case down, we need to find out what's going on and then set up a situation where I can expose it. I know the boss woman is running some sort of drugs. I know that they are in graves which are unmarked at Calgary Bay but what I don't know is the connection between Keir and her, and if there is one, why there is one. Was Keir tied up in this drug racket somehow? Because at the moment, I'm not sure how.

The boys on the *Sandra Jane* are obviously involved but was Keir with them and did something go wrong? And as I've always said, surely if they thought they needed to get rid of him, they'd just toss him overboard; they'd be out in the water plenty and why would they make such a public statement? If she knew they were involved and knew who they were, she'd go and visit them to scare them, not simply dump a dead mate knowing that the authorities would come in to look. Something about this isn't right. And how did Keir get involved? All I know is he's got photographs of himself with the Asian girl and she's a lot happier in them than she is in any of Jack Doolan's. Sitting in the car, I outline all this Susan and ask her what she thinks.

'We can't go back to the drug dealers—they just want us dead,' she says, 'Keir is dead as well. We can't go to the drug site because that'll expose what we know, and the drug dealers will probably run. So, the only line of attack as I see it are the boys on the *Sandra Jane*. We need to find out from them what's going on from their side.'

'Spot on,' I say, 'and that means we may need to rough it up a bit but be careful because these are not amateur idiots. If they've been nicking drugs off people and looking to move them on, they'll have something about them, so we tread carefully. But we go in hard as I think we've possibly got a day or two to clear this up. After that, more and more people further away from here could get put in danger. At the moment the drugs are still there and they'll be scared that we've tipped somebody off. So, they're going to watch and wait to see if the police come after them before they cut and run. So yeah, it's time to shake down our boat crew and find out what they know.'

Chapter Seventeen

I've pulled a wig from my bag of tricks for Susan. I've got a large hat and sunglasses on myself trying to make us look just somewhat different. Rather than drive around to the house of the boys from the *Sandra Jane*, we decide instead to go to Tobermory, place ourselves inside a coffee shop, and keep an eye out the window to see them arrive for the boat. I have a funny feeling they'll be round sometime because that's what they seem to do.

Sure enough, around about mid-morning on the day following on from us catching our ferry, they show up. We've had a rough night sleeping in the car so my mood isn't great, and neither is Susan's, but you can tell she's a little bit excited by this hunt. She's doing what she really wanted, finally getting a chance to go on a real case with all the danger. It's not perfect and I've told her she needs to really listen to me this time but we'll see how we go.

I see the tall figure of Andrew, the blond hair bouncing as he strides onto his boat. Together, I walk arm in arm with Susan along the shoreline looking to the pontoons where the boat is berthed. Digsy and John seem to have been sent off for something, possibly supplies and so I station Susan at the end of the pontoons as I make my way down towards the boat.

Andrew is at the rear of it, working on some sort of engine, and I creep onto the front, hiding on one side of the deck waiting for him to make his way back to the front.

It's not the largest of boats but there is room and as he makes his way forward, I'm able to open up a hatch and get into the bow of the boat. Soon I hear the three of them come back on board and I assume the boat's making its way out of Tobermory harbour. I give myself twenty minutes before I pop my head up, much to the surprise of all three of them. You may think I've snookered myself with this one, a one-armed man with three of them out in the water. Surely, they won't entertain me; they could simply knock me out and dump my body. But I didn't come without packing firepower.

'What the hell are you doing?' says Andrew, recognizing me immediately. 'I don't get it, Mr. What are you sneaking aboard our boat for?' I clamber up as the other two lads surround me. 'Well, I'm waiting for an answer,' said Andrew. 'You pay if you want to come out in this boat.'

'Do you know the name Keir Matheson,' I say calmly and slowly. There's a brief meeting of eyes as Andrew and John look at each other. They think they're doing it surreptitiously but it's pretty obvious. Digsy seems to shake a little and move away from me, his cheeky grin having gone, giving his ginger-haired face a more sinister glare.

'Never heard of him,' said Andrew. 'What are you doing here? And who is this guy?'

I can't be arsed with this. I need to get the bottom of what's happening and so from behind my back pull out my gun. It has the effect to cause the three of them to step back, Digsy nearly falling overboard and the boat rocks a little. This doesn't bother me as I've had sea legs develop on the years of being on

CHAPTER SEVENTEEN

my boat and I keep the gun down by my side, making sure no other boats can see it. 'I don't care what else you're up to, lads. All I want to know is about Keir Matheson. I know he came and worked on your boat.'

'Who told you that?'

'Keir did,' I say but I have no idea that he really did. We simply followed their boat round from Gometra where Keir was found dead. I saw them plant the drugs; I saw them bring them back. Keir must have been involved with them; otherwise, he wouldn't have been dead and now I have seen their eyes, I definitely know he was with them. I also know, listening to them at their shed, that he's a problem to them. But I don't want them to know I've been watching.

'I need answers, boys, and I need them fast and then you turn around, I get off this boat, and you don't see me again. But if you don't answer, then our trip becomes longer. Maybe some of you don't make it back ashore.'

I don't tell them about the drugs, what I know and maybe they think I'm involved with it—maybe I'm the hit man for the drug smugglers. I don't say because I want them to think of every possibility and I want them to tremble.

'Look, mister,' says Andrew, 'we had nothing to do with what happened to Keir.'

'Are you sure about that?' I ask him. 'He wasn't left in a good way, maybe the four of you had a falling out.'

'No, that's just the way we found him,' said Digsy. 'Look, mister, we didn't touch Keir—he was just dead; they just found him dead.'

'But he was working with you guys, wasn't he? So, what do you know about him?' I ask.

'Are you a cop?' asks John. 'Are you the fuzz?'

'Would I be the police if I were holding a gun to you?' I say. 'I'm a man who wants answers. Someone's paying me to get them and this is just business, boys. You look like a nice group of people but I know what I need and I need to go away from here with it because if I don't, I'm going to have to take those answers from you, one way or another.'

'Hey, easy,' says Digsy, 'easy. We can tell you what you want, can't we, Andrew? We can tell him. Andy, tell him.'

'Keir did some work with us, a pleasure-cruise-type thing, needed a spare hand on board.' Andrew's playing it very cool, not giving anything away about the drugs but I let him continue to talk. 'He just called up one morning, said to us he had to go. I knew he was working with that Doolan guy who does the photographs and he called off on us saying he had to go down to Inch Kenneth to photograph something. He'd done it a couple of times, said it was important to keep that job. I told him we needed him but he said he needed to do it, something more important than money. That was his phrase.'

'Yes,' said John. 'He said that a lot, that all the money wouldn't have made a difference, no matter how much we got.'

'Shut it,' said Andrew. 'You don't need to talk about that.'

I bring the gun out a little bit further pointing it at Andrew. 'You don't need to talk about what, sunshine?' I say. 'Tell me the lot.'

'Keir was just involved in a few ventures of ours that might bring in a bit of money, that's all.' You can understand they're a little bit underhand, so we don't like to talk about them but that's all. But he said he was off to Inch Kenneth. How he got from there to end up being naked and dead on Gometra, I don't know, sir.'

It's *sir* now. Not often I get called that, but it is nice and

CHAPTER SEVENTEEN

at least he's being respectful of the gun. 'Do you guys have anything to do with Gometra?' Again, there's a shift of eyes from John to Andrew.

'Nothing,' said Andrew, 'of course we know where it is, of course we pass it; there's a few crab fishermen round there. You get the pots put down, done a few of that myself in this time, otherwise got nothing to do with it. Don't even know anybody living on it.'

'Did Keir say anything about the photographer he was working with on this other job?'

'No,' said Andrew. 'He hardly spoke about it, just said the important things.'

I notice Digsy is looking very sheepish. He's got one of those faces that has plenty to hide. 'You,' I call, 'what do you know? You know something else, don't you?'

'No, I don't, sir. I know nothing, nothing at all.'

'Come over here,' I say and watch as the boy slowly makes his way across. As he reaches me, I swipe across his face, connecting with his chin. It's a hard smack and a little bit of blood draws out of the side of his mouth. 'Don't piss me about,' I say. 'Tell me what he's told you. Next time it won't be the butt of the gun.'

He's holding his chin and I can see he was about to swear, but he's afraid of me, which frankly, is good. I do feel a little for him because I think he's disposable to these two even though he doesn't know it.

'Look, mister,' he said, 'just take it easy. Keir had a girl, cracking-looking girl too—used to show me some photographs he took of her.' I note the shock on the faces of Andrew and John because this is something they didn't share.

'Go on,' I say, 'what else did he tell you about her?'

'He did show me a couple of the pics. She's a cracker, way above his league,' he said, 'and he got to photograph her. That was something he said, said she liked being photographed by him, told me how he took her along picnics and that and they'd spend a couple of hours together. I tried to push him on whether or not he bagged her. He was pretty candid and I think he . . . I think he had made it with her which frankly quite stunned me.'

'What did this girl look like?'

'Asian,' says Digsy, 'not that I normally hold with Asian girls but she was a looker, good set on her too, at least that's what it looked like from the photograph. You can't tell, can you, some of these model types?'

It's all a bit crass but at least he's giving the information that I want. 'And he's was off to meet her, in Inch Kenneth?'

'I think he wanted more than that. I think they were planning something,' says Digsy.

'Well, where did she live then?' I say. 'She used to come to him,' replies Digsy, 'always met up; he never said where she lived but she was on the island. It's actually quite a sad story, quite poor in a lot of ways which I find quite hard because the photographs he had of her when she was clothed, she was wearing some quite stunning stuff, proper gear, cost a bit.'

'How the hell would you know?' said Andrew. 'Come to the isles out of nowhere.'

'Shut up,' says Digsy. 'I know class when I see it and she was class.'

'Can't be that much class if she's getting her kit off the whole time,' says John.

I feel this conversation is running away from me and so I wave the gun about a bit and tell the boys to quieten down.

CHAPTER SEVENTEEN

'Now listen to me, gents. I was never here and you didn't hear from me. If my name is ever spoken to anyone else or a description of me surfaces, I will come and I will find you, and the way Keir was left will be nothing as to the way you're found. Turn the boat back in the harbour and drop me off.'

Andrew spins the boat right and we spend an uncomfortable twenty minutes before we get back into the harbour. As we arrive, Susan clocks me approaching but Andrew is also perceptive and spots her despite her different-coloured hair. 'Is she working for you?' he says. 'Have you been watching us the whole time?'

'I have been watching you and not only with her.' This of course is an outright lie, but I want them to look around them desperately trying to find anyone who just looks a little bit strange and off. 'Remember,' I say as I step off the boat, 'I will find you if you mention me, or any of my associates. You guys might be out of your league on this one.' With the gun packed away, I step off the boat and walk up the harbour to join Susan at the top.

'That go all right, Paddy?'

'Yes' I say, 'it appears Keir was heading off to Inch Kenneth the day he disappeared but we need to know why. He was also deeply involved with the Asian lady which we kind of guessed from the photographs. But to get from Inch Kenneth over to Gometra, you'll take him on a boat. You'd either have to abduct him out there or you'll have to knock him out in some way to travel. Either way, it'd be hard for someone to haul a body up unto Gometra in the middle of the night.'

'Do you think those guys on the boat had anything to do with it?'

I shake my head. 'Doubtful. I really turned on them. And the

Digsy guy, he just blubbered. I'm wondering if we're looking at something vastly different. Sarah Hunstanton was employed to check out Doolan by his wife which makes me wonder what she knew about him. What made her suspect? Yes, he's got a lock on the door. But there must be something else. I think we need to have a word with Annie, need to find out what angle she's coming from because this may not be about the drugs at all. '

Susan looks at me and I can see in her mind the thoughts churning. 'She is a heck of a good-looking woman, isn't she, Paddy? I mean if you fell for her, if you're meeting her, taking her places, photographing her like that, do you think you would have run with her?'

'I think there's two things we need to do,' I say. 'I need to talk to Annie Doolan and find out her side of the story. But I also need to talk to our Asian lady—let's see her side. Annie Doolan should be fairly easy to reach. How we get a hold of our Asian woman, that's something else entirely.'

Chapter Eighteen

I'm unsure as to whether or not Annie Doolan will be being watched. One of the problems I have at the moment, being a marked man, is that the people I was investigating and the people concerned in this case may be being watched by the smugglers and if I simply barge in to find these people, then I could have difficulty. The first thing we do is make our way round towards the Doolan house. I can see a car sitting not far from it with two large goons inside. Yes, the car is a different one than I've seen parked at the house where the smugglers are based but you'd recognize those goons anywhere. They're sitting with a couple of ice lollies, licking them as if they're meant to be two tourists out and about, but rarely do you see two six-foot-two tourists with shoulders wider than a shipyard plonked eating ice lollies in black suits. If that's what's come to the Isle of Mull, its clientele has distinctly changed in the time that I've known it. So, they're not that clever but that doesn't mean they're not deadly.

I let Susan drop me off further away and tell her to keep driving around. I'll give her a call when I'm ready to be picked up. I don't go in any particular disguise but make my way through the back fields to the rear of the Doolan house. I can see the expensive car that Annie Doolan likes to drive around in, and with my binoculars I see her occasionally appearing at the windows. Jack Doolan's inside as well and there's a distinct coolness between the couple. In fact, at one point, there's a row and he tries to put his arms around her but she throws him off. I can't read a lot more through the window as generally she's turned away from me.

He's apologizing, saying sorry, and occasionally asking what she means. When she does turn round, she says a couple of words that, frankly, my mother wouldn't like me saying and she also states what she'll do to him if he's cheating on her. Suffice to say, he'd be singing exceedingly high for the forthcoming weeks. Maybe she's getting a bit bothered as well though, because her investigator has just disappeared off island and I told Sarah Hunstanton not to contact anyone until I could close down the case. That's a basis I can meet her on.

Her car is parked round the rear of the house and it's out of sight of the goons. Grabbing a pencil and piece of paper, I make a note before running up to the car which I find to be unlocked. This is handy as I wasn't sure I could break in but opening the door quickly, I leave a note tucked into a glasses case housing a pair of shades that she must use for driving.

I tell her to meet me at the Ulva ferry one hour after she finds this note then I step back to sit and watch the car, waiting for it to hopefully leave the house that day. I'm not disappointed when towards teatime, she makes her way out. I see her put on the glasses and read the note. She looks around her, but on not seeing anyone, drives off. I have to trust that she thinks Sarah has written the note.

I make my way back through the fields and meet up again with Susan and take the car down to the Ulva ferry. I send Susan across the narrow passage telling her to sit and watch

CHAPTER EIGHTEEN

from the other side. I also ask her to scope out and see if there's anybody resembling a six-foot-two thug on that side and if there is, to phone back across.

Annie Doolan is right on time. She stops her flash vehicle in the car park beside the ferry and steps out looking around, no doubt for Sarah Hunstanton. I walk casually over towards her when she glances at me before looking away. 'I think we need to get on the ferry,' I say. 'Sarah says.'

The woman looks at me, tilts her chin to the sky, her hair set in waves and then turns looking at me through her sunglasses. 'You, Paddy Smythe, the investigator?' she asks.

'A little lie of sorts. Working for your investigator, Miss Hunstanton; she can't break cover at the moment but she wanted me to talk to you. She has a few other questions. Let's take a trip over on the ferry—it's quieter over there.' The woman looks around again before turning and walking to the ferry, leaving me standing where I am. I give her about twenty seconds before joining her as the ferry arrives. I pay and make my way across, not talking to her and staying on the other side of the boat, albeit a small boat as it is. On the other side, Susan meets her off the ferry and directs her to a small table. I disappear inside and come back with a couple of pints, carrying them on a small tray, a feat which seems to impress Annie Doolan.

'When did you lose your arm?' she says to me, as if making small talk.

'That's not important,' I say. 'What is important is your husband. You contacted Sarah, I believe, because you thought he may be cheating on you.'

This seems like a fairly obvious statement. I'm expecting her just to nod but the woman takes off her glasses and dabs her eyes.'

'Do you know what he said to me today? He said to me I'd lost my figure, said to me he could find better. He used to beg me, want me to be in his pictures and I did. I posed for him but he wanted seedier things. I never realized when I married him he had no class but he never did anything; he was a coward, up till now. He's up to something. Tell me, what has Sarah found?'

'It's not that simple,' I say. 'We need to work out if anything else unusual has been happening. Have you noticed anything odd, anything strange? Not with him but with you?' I ask.

'How do you mean?' she says.

'With your work, have you ever noticed anything go missing, anything unusual happening. I take it you have access to a large number of drugs.'

'Of course,' she says, 'and all signed out. When I'm in London I have access down there. I also have access with the GP surgery here because sometimes I'm called to administer from here. Exceedingly small place and I'm on the rotation for cover. It's a little bit below my level of expertise but hey, I try to be part of this community.' She flicks her head back as if begging me to affirm her in that respect.

'Very good yourself,' I say, 'but tell me, has there been anything strange around outside of it?'

'Why? Do you think he's in bed with one of my colleagues, one of the people I work with?'

'That's always a possibility,' I say, although I don't believe a word of what I've just said. 'But they may be doing something for a reason too, pulling him in. Has there been any unusual activity?'

'I can't really think of anything,' she said. 'Down in London with a little bit of trouble on the ward, a man coming in when

CHAPTER EIGHTEEN

he shouldn't have been there. But the police had a word and he just seemed to be possibly schizophrenic. Then that patient died the other week, and their relatives were upset; it got a little bit violent but that's nothing unusual. On this end, there's been nothing. We lost a couple of drugs, but it was basic stuff.'

'What do you mean basic stuff?' I ask.

'Just things to numb people, it could even knock them out for a bit. It's used normally to numb your bones but there was a significant degree taken.'

'Enough to stun someone, enough to make him unable to defend himself?'

Her eyes are raised this time. 'Why? Why would someone want to do that? What's that got to do with my husband running off with a woman? Is he a sort of date rapist?' she says. 'Do you think he's drugging them? It's not actually an affair at all?'

'It's one of the possibilities we're looking at,' I say keen to make her think I have a reasonable suspicion about what's going on but it is good news, something tangible, something that says he could have knocked Keir out. He could have killed him without having to fight him, stab him, or wound him. Keir was found dead with a remarkably simple nick to his throat. He died being unable to breathe but there was not a lot of blood and I hear of a method that could have been used to do that but why? Could it just be sheer jealousy?

I need to understand the relationship between Doolan and the girl. What did he think he had with her? What did he think he was going to get? If he realized that Keir was moving in on her, did he know what they had planned; did he understand what was going on between them? It's an understanding that I don't have.

'If he's done something like that to women, to anyone,' says Annie Doolan, 'throw the damn book at him.'

'Oh, we will,' says Susan taking a lead I wasn't expecting. 'But until we can prove it, you need to stay quiet and you need to stick to behaving like there's nothing wrong.'

'Nothing wrong?' she says, 'I had a row with him today. He knows I think he's cheating on me.'

'That's fine,' I say. 'But don't let any of what we've told you come out. Don't mention this slight drug loss but I want to know how he could get access. Do you have keys to where these things would be stored?'

The woman nods. 'I've got my emergency set in case I'm called in the middle of the night. But I have to clock out everything I use, it has to be noted, dispensed and if I gave it to anyone else, I'd have to make note of it as well. We keep tight lists—that's how we know something was missing.'

'Was it simply a full bottle that was taken?'

'All that was left,' she says, 'it was way too much of a dose; you could have knocked somebody out with it, but this dose would have had them sleeping for a long time. You could have managed to knock them unconscious with a quarter of it. Do you think my husband is taking it in large doses because he's operating with a lot of women? Have there been reports to the police?' she says.

'It's a line we're taking,' says Susan, following my earlier lead. 'But like we say, we haven't got anything concrete yet so don't mention it. Just keep on going the way you are and we'll be back in touch soon.'

The ferry's back over this side and together, the three of us make our way back across. As we drop her off back at the car, I shake her hand and tell her that Sarah will be in touch soon

CHAPTER EIGHTEEN

and not to worry, we'll soon have her husband exposed for what he is. She doesn't know what that means which is fine by me. As we watch her drive away, Susan puts a hand on my shoulder. 'So, do you think you know what's going on, Paddy?' she says. 'Do you think Doolan killed Keir?'

'I do,' I say. 'I really do but how to prove it. By the time they found him, I don't know there's anything left in his system to indicate he'd been knocked out. They know his throat had been slit but with what? There's no murder weapon. There's no way of getting in there. He was meant to be in Inch Kenneth but to call the police back in now means re-interviewing everyone there, trying to find tourists, trying to build up a case against Doolan. I'm not sure it's going to fly.'

'So, what are you going to do?' she asks.

'I'll do what I always do. If you can't serve up justice with the police, it will have to be taken in another way and besides, we need to bring down these smugglers as well. They are all over our backs; they're all over Sarah Hunstanton's as well. We won't be clear until we can get them away from us which means we need to blow their operation to do that. I'm going to need to know a little bit more about it. There's one person who can tell us but she is going to be damn hard to get hold of.'

'Who?' asks Susan.

'That Asian girl. I think she wanted a way out and I think that's why she was with Keir. Well, let's give her a route out; let's find her and give her a route out.'

'How are you going to do that?' she asks me.

'Oh, I'm not,' I say; 'you are.' There's a mix of excitement and fear on Susan's face but as we get back in the car, I see her fists and they pump slightly as she realizes she's going to be at the forefront of this deception.

'Thank you, Paddy,' she says as she gets in the car.

'Don't thank me yet. If you realize the risk you're about to run, you may never thank me again.'

Chapter Nineteen

What we're about to do depends a lot on Susan. Over the last while I've put her through quite a bit of training, tried to teach her how to stay smart on her feet out of sight, but now she's going to have to be herself, very much in sight and then get on the move. She's going to have to put into effect all the training I gave her about evading capture because I'm going to offer her up as bait. But in order to do that, and to do it at a sensible time, I need to first find out when the next photographs are going to be taken. Our favourite smuggler doesn't know we're back; neither does Jack Doolan. The boys on the boat do but they're not going to contact either of these people because they still want to remain anonymous so that they can pick up their other drugs.

There's also one other side to this I'm not quite sure about—how the guys on the boat stumbled upon the drugs, how they got involved. I have a suspicion and it involves Keir and certain photographs he was taking with the young Asian lady. I'd like to say it's a hunch because that sounds rather dramatic. It's a bit more than that; it's more intuitive and it's backed up by a lack of ideas of how else the boys in the boat got involved. They don't seem like proper smugglers and they've walked in and taken away drugs from some people who if they find out will try to kill them on the spot. Not very clever when you're pedalling in a small boat like that.

I also think the boys on the boat are running slightly scared; hence the fact that Andrew and John are looking to ditch Digsy as soon as they get their drugs to move on and I wonder where they'll move them on, probably selling some top-class-geek gear to next-to-nobody on the street for a fraction of its value. I don't mind as at the end of this, they all get nabbed, put behind bars. But the last thing I want to see is any of those boys getting killed so I have to play this right.

Our first stop is surveillance on Jack Doolan. His wife Annie has left for London again, and this is always a good sign for when Jack gets up to his other activities. It's later when we finally see him make a move. He loads his photographic gear into the back of his car and drives off. I've been banking that our head smuggler won't lose her appetite for these pictures that Jack provides and it seems it may be the case as Jack disappears through the Mull countryside, eventually stopping a long way from a beach, one we've been to before.

Susan's in the car with me, armed with a very obvious camera but it's not time to reveal our hand yet and the two of us have parked our hire car some distance from Jack Doolan's. We make our way over towards the beach, hiding high up above it as the man sets up below. He goes through the usual routine, getting some lighting gear together and it's then I hear the boat.

Once again, she's sat at the front of it with a large coat on and this time two bodyguards on the boat. They bring the small craft up to the beach where she jumps out and walks without looking back at them over to Jack Doolan. He smiles, says a few words to her and very matter-of-factly, she removes the jacket. She's wearing some, how would we put it, fantasy gear

CHAPTER NINETEEN

underneath, dressed up to look like, I think, an elf but one who's got a rather low clothing budget. Clearly our handsome ogre has got some imagination but soon they're into taking the photographs and my eyes are on the bodyguards sat just off the water.

It's two hours before I see the photography shoot about to slow down and I send Susan off, trying to watch the beach, and telling her to keep in sight until our young Asian lady starts to walk away. As she makes her way across the beach and is about to get into the boat, Susan, making sure her red hair is draped out with the large camera in front of her, stands on the beach, taking photographs of the woman getting into the boat. I hear a cry and one of the bodyguards gets out and starts running after Susan. Doolan's face is a picture as he recognizes who she is and he begins to pack up quickly.

Susan hightails it back up the small cliff face and starts making her way across the moor. I wait until I see the other bodyguards shouting back and the man in the boat starts to tail him, setting off making his way round the coastline, they are obviously hoping to cut Susan off. It's a bad plan because you can't cut inland, and I trust she's going to be quick.

The Asian woman is left on the beach, wrapped up in a coat, and she sits down looking rather fed up. Doolan ignores her and having got his gear, makes his way back up the cliff face and heads for his car. At this point I make my way down, keeping out of sight of everyone until I'm sure no one can see me on the beach. Moving along behind some rocks, I call out gently to the woman who turns and looks transfixed on my single arm.

'You were in the house,' she says. 'Why did you come back? They'll kill you.'

'I know,' I say, 'but I'm here because of Keir.' Her face looks like it's about to erupt with emotion and I see tears are starting to come into her eyes.

'Why do you bring that name up? Keir's dead; he got too close, too involved, and they killed him.'

'I don't think they did,' I say. I think Keir was killed by Jack Doolan.'

She looks at me. 'Who's Jack Doolan?'

'The man who has just been shooting you for the last two hours.'

'No, that's Ian. Keir was staying with Ian.'

'Did Keir tell you he was Ian?'

I see her look at me thoughtfully, turn away for a moment and then back. 'No,' she says, 'he never did. I never asked him—that man's always been Ian to me. I don't think I ever called him by name in front of Keir.'

'The man's Jack Doolan and I think he has a rather soft spot for you. He seems to get a lot more pleasure out of what he's doing than a professional photographer would. He keeps your photographs in a basement of his that's locked from his wife. But tell me how you and Keir got so involved and how did he manage to meet you for photographs?'

'Before we start that, who are you?' she says.

'I'm here because of Keir's mother. She asked me to find out what happened to her son. My name is Paddy and that's all you need to know so far except that I think I can get you out of this. I take it you're not here by choice.' The woman shakes her head. 'My associate is going to keep those men away but it'll probably only be for a short time, so I need you to answer my questions and answer them quick. And then we shall try and get you over the next day or two away from them and off

CHAPTER NINETEEN

to some new life somewhere else.'

'Why should I believe you?' she says. 'Everyone just takes from me. Maybe you just want to take me away, use me.'

I shake my head. 'I don't think the woman sitting back in my boat would take too kindly to that and neither will her daughter who's currently running around keeping your goons at bay. So, tell me, how did you and Keir manage to do it and what was the plan?'

'Can I trust you Paddy?'

'If you want to get out of here, you're going to have to,' I say. 'It's your choice but I'm going to bring them down and I'm going to involve the police. I'd rather not involve the police with you. I'd rather move you away on your own and set you up somewhere else.'

I see her give it a moment's thought but then she turns to me, nodding, saying, 'Okay then, Keir followed Ian out, spied on him shooting me one day. Ian was in a hurry and my guards were late back; something had happened, but Keir came down to the beach to see me. We had maybe half an hour to an hour. He was besotted with me and those eyes of a young man, probably driven more by his hormones than anything else,' she says. 'I thought I could get out. I hear a lot being at the bed of Atlanta—that's the boss, that's who's running the operation. You've met her, she was the one torturing you.' I nod my head. I remember that too well.

'I told Keir that I would run away with him and in honesty I would have if it had come off. I know about the drugs. I told him where they were, told him to get some friends and to steal some, then one day we will run off together. They had quite a few of the drugs taken, I believe, but they got to him before we could go—they killed him and left him on the other island.'

'How did you keep in contact with Keir though?' I say.

'Ian would always tell me when we would next meet. All the detail came through me, so it was easy saying what I had to do and when. I would get dropped off and my guards didn't care who was taking photographs of me so Keir would come along and do them. We would talk as I stood there posing. If my guards disappeared, he would bring lunch as well and then he would go back onto Doolan's equipment and send photographs. He would find the account, find where they were meant to go. But Atlanta must have found out and she stopped him—found out about the drugs.'

'No, she didn't,' I say. 'I don't think she even knows about Keir. I believe Jack Doolan, or Ian as you call him, killed Keir. I believe it's because he was jealous of you and Keir. I think he knew you were going to run. He took some drugs from his wife, things that would knock Keir out, then dispatched him because he knew where Keir was going as he was working, learning and training from him.

Keir also got involved with a boat allegedly to do some part-time work. The boys on the boat have been stealing the drugs from the graves at Calgary Bay, hiding them on an island called Gometra. They're on a boat called the *Sandra Jane*. I need you to tell me when the next drugs are going to be found and delivered to the graves at Calgary. When you know that I'll tip the boys in and then I'll tip the police to find them all. I'll make it look like Doolan's told them, so Atlanta thinks Doolan's done it. And once the cops pick everybody up, I'll get you out and I'll get you away somewhere else completely and you can start a life again.'

'And what will I owe you for that?' she says. 'Will my life be with you?'

CHAPTER NINETEEN

I shake my head. 'You won't owe me anything; you'll have given me what I need. I was here to prove that Keir was killed, murdered, here to catch his killers but I can't do it. I can't get the evidence together that holds up. So instead I'm going to make sure he gets justice. You'll have given that to me. Setting you up elsewhere, it'll be my pleasure. If it all goes to plan, Atlanta and the rest of her boys won't be coming out of a cell for ten to fifteen years along with Jack Doolan if he survives it. Here,' I say, and hand her a SIM card. 'Do you have a phone?'

The woman nods. 'I have it for contacting, letting them know when we're done here.'

'Good,' I say. 'Keep that SIM card safe. They can't trace it to me but there's one number on it. Text all the details to that number . . . what and when the drugs are coming, on which night and then break the SIM card, flush it away down the toilet, do something with it, get rid of it and don't worry, the communication at the other end will be destroyed as well. Then I'll be in touch to come and get you. And now I'm going to go,' I say. 'By the way, you know I'm Paddy. What's your name? First name only,' I say.

'Leah,' she says, and her eyes begin to well up. 'I didn't mean for Keir to get . . . well, you know,' she says.

'I know,' I say, 'and you didn't get him killed. One jealous man got him killed and if he hadn't been so keen on you, I think your plan might have worked, but this one will. Find out, don't push for it just when you hear, and I'll be in touch.' I don't look back but head up the cliff side secluding myself high up above. About ten minutes later I get a message from Susan. She says she's clear and hiding and gives me her GPS location. She's about two miles away inside a forest and so I make my way back to the car, drive around, stopping some distance away and scan the area. One of the goons is there still looking, but he's some distance off where she is. I make my way in, kneeling down beside Susan without her even realizing that I've arrived.

'Your lookout's crap,' I say. 'I just walked in; you never even noticed me.' She goes to speak, but I put my hand up against her mouth. 'Not here, this way,' I say. I make a way back to the car and then we drive off to the south side of Mull. Martha's managed to hire us a caravan on a private site down there, but my intention is not to do anything until I get that call, let everyone think we've been scared off. So that night over a glass of wine, I congratulate Susan as she tells me about her escape, running from the goons turning this way and that, never letting them get within five hundred yards of her. But as she speaks, my mind's going through the options, the permutations of what could happen. This will be the hardest part, waiting for the information but I think Leah is going to be good for it. There was a weariness in her eyes, but she was brave enough to take on Keir to get out; he was a mere lad. Hopefully, in me, she has seen someone who might give her a bit more hope.

Chapter Twenty

It took four days, four days of sitting around a caravan, four days of hearing Susan talk about the music she likes. It's music from a younger generation and like those of us in the older generation, I think it's all rubbish. Well, maybe not all but they really don't know a good tune. Four days of looking at the inside of a caravan, stretching my legs very occasionally. The good news is that nothing untoward was happening further south. Martha kept an eye on Maggie and Kirsten, and nothing had been traced to them so far, either that or they were just being cautious. There's no point shaking up people unless you think you can reach the person you're trying to get at through them.

Hans is recovering but he wasn't feeling the best. Lorraine is still taking care of him at the private address we have and although he'll take time to recover, he's good. Unfortunately, he's out of action at a time when I really could have done with him but Susan has proved her worth when she gave those guards the run-around and now, she's going to have to prove it again. The text message comes in very simply.

'drop on. tomorrow night. arriving 2am. photography shoot arranged. Doolan's. midnight onwards.'

Leah obviously has sense; she knows I have to get her away

and the easiest place to do that is when she was with Doolan. I told her I'd bring the police in and that I will, but she's also given me a place to go and grab her.

Sitting at the table inside our caravan, I've got a pen and paper and I've sketched out a small map of the area. It's rough but at least it's something. Doolan's house is close to Calgary Bay so I think we can operate easily enough. Susan's going to do the grab, get hold of Leah and get her out of there. When I get the call, I ring Maggie and Martha. Kirsten and herself are already on their way up in *Craigantlet*, my boat. That's where Leah's going once we get her clear and then when she's with Martha, Martha will take her somewhere that I won't know.

One of the things about Martha is, of all my contacts, I know the least about her. Yes, I know who she is and what she does. I know her past, too, but I don't know her present. I've never asked questions and I know that she keeps a low profile. When we talk about our life, we talk about it very generically—the AA meeting she goes to, the church badminton club. Could be anywhere. Everything I have talked about with her gives no indication of where she actually lives. And so, if I want someone to disappear, Martha does it because then if anyone comes after me, I haven't got a clue where they are.

The tricky bit is to get the boys there and with that in mind, I'm going to tell them 'I want recompense for Keir's mom and so I want the drugs. They're going to go and pick them up for me.' So, the plan's quite simple, or as simple as these things ever get: drugs arrive, the boys pick them up, but won't be aware our smugglers will be watching and protecting their stash. The boys will arrive, and the smugglers will see them. Everybody else won't be aware but I'll have tipped off the police who'll be watching already so everyone gets grabbed. Susan grabs Leah

CHAPTER TWENTY

while all this is going on, takes her off to *Craigantlet*. I drop a few things to make sure Doolan's implicated, hopefully get him along to the scene and he gets picked up as well. And everyone thinks that Leah has done a runner and was looking to go with Doolan who came back for the drugs and got caught.

We'll make sure there's some nice letters, some handwriting from Leah, indicating the plan. She'll obviously be portrayed as a pawn in the whole thing. The key is making sure that the police come because what have I got to actually offer them at the moment? I could tell them where the drugs are but then they'd be there before all this went into play. So, I need to make sure that the tip I give is in place. We're also on Mull which is not the easiest place to simply pour a lot of policemen into quickly. And so, I think we'll need to make sure that a proper surveillance is done on this.

I ring an old contact and I tell him that a source is going to be ringing tonight confidentially and he probably wants to have a word with those who are on the Drug Squad to make sure they go with this one because it's a good tip. When the rather dour-faced Lewis man asks me what I've got to do with this, I simply tell him that somebody came for advice. My advice was to ring in confidence and let the force deal with it. I'm not sure if he believed me but he'll pass it on. The trouble with someone like Macleod is that he is very by-the-book, and the trouble with what I'm dealing with is by-the-book so often doesn't work.

We leave the caravan in darkness on the night of the drop and the weather's closed in. The rain started that afternoon, but it hasn't ceased since and I hope it's not going to affect the photography shoot that's meant to be happening. If Leah has any wit, she'll make sure it goes ahead even if it's just to get there and tell him it's off.

We park the car four miles away and make across country to the rear of Doolan's house. As we get close, I look around just to make sure there's no surveillance but why would there be? Surveillance will be on the graves. I placed the call, the anonymous call, to the confidential line that afternoon which meant it was tight for them to get full surveillance in place, but there should be enough for what's going to happen. I got to the boys that afternoon too, caught them down at Tobermory harbour where they were met by a two-armed man in a large overcoat who explained to them what they were doing that night and that if they didn't, he would soon explain to someone else where they were and the fact that they had drugs belonging to somebody.

Chapter Twenty-One

The boys were already making their plans when I left them; let's hope they come through.

I sit for half an hour with Susan. It's just after ten o'clock; the rain's piling down but that doesn't bother us as we're intently focused on the comings and goings of the Doolan house. Annie's not there and I can see a canopy being built in the trees behind the house. Jack Doolan's been back and forward and he has some rather strange items out with him. There's a sword, there's some sort of chainmail armour of a warrior, definitely a female warrior, but it seems to lack a lot of protective areas. I guess it's whatever floats your boat but this is all good news for us because things are going ahead. I leave Susan in position, keeping an eye and I make my way round towards the graves at Calgary Bay, which are less than half a mile away.

As I start to get close, I take it very slowly. With my infrared goggles, I'm able to pick out some surveillance in the distance. In fairness, it's not that obvious and it's quite wide out because they don't know exactly where these graves are. I can count at least six people watching, most of them are hidden in the grass but there's a van parked in a house further up. I reckon that's police as well, probably using the house as the operations base.

As for me, I'm going to sit tight because I don't see the point in getting too close. The drop's not until two so I make my way back to Susan and right on midnight, we see a black car driving to Doolan's.

Out steps Leah, welcomed by Jack Doolan and taken round to the rear of the house. The car then drives off and sure enough, ten minutes later, Leah is posing for Jack wearing whatever on earth that outfit was he had for her. I tell Susan to keep an eye and I'll be back.

Moving back to the main arena, I'm sat in my hidey hole, a distance away for at least an hour and a half. It's then, with the infrared goggles, I can see a boat coming into the bay, a single person gets off and walks over to the grave, the one that sits away from the marked graves. He starts to dig and roll back the ground. A small package is put inside, the person looks around him, checking for anyone and then kneels down quietly out of the way when a car passes on the main road. He packs everything away and disappears off again.

There will have been lots of photographs and this person will now be being tailed. I dare say there's a boat out on the water or maybe some drone following them. But it's just after that a car pulls up on the main road and a young lad runs out over to the grave. He has a spade in hand and it's all incredibly amateur.

The boys are obviously spooked, so they haven't come in on the boat but rather just arrived by car to dig things up. As the man's digging, I see figures move to surround him. The man's grabbed, the car intercepted at the roadside and the boys have been apprehended. Hopefully, they're now looking to apprehend the boat, but the mobile vibrates in my pocket. I take it out and quickly look, it's a message from Susan saying

CHAPTER TWENTY-ONE

she has complications. The black car's just arrived and Atlanta, the smuggling boss, has just stepped out.

I make my way quickly back toward Susan's position, telling her to sit tight as the last thing she needs is to be involved. When I get there, she's been a good girl and not moved at all but she's shaking because Atlanta has Jack Doolan on his knees, hands tied behind his back. Beside him, her hands also tied back, but still in her ridiculous outfit is Leah.

Atlanta has a gun on either side, pointing at their heads. She's asking Jack what's going on? Why have her drugs been grabbed? Why are the police here? I'm not sure if she suspects Leah but what she does know is that I've been round here, other people have been round Doolan's asking questions and no doubt, I've also been around Tobermory, which is where some boys have just been grabbed come from. Atlanta is clutching at straws, not knowing what's going on and in fairness, she's a lot more astute than Doolan probably realizes. But he's giving the performance of his life saying he knows nothing, which he does.

But now she's asking questions about Keir, about the lad that was murdered. She says she knows that Keir lived here, worked here, so she has been keeping her tabs on Doolan. I wonder at which point she'll shoot him.

Atlanta is now over at Leah, gun pressed firm into her jaw but you can see the attraction as well. She's leering at Leah, seems to have a fascination with her. Leah's spinning a yarn, a yarn about how Doolan was threatening her, used Keir as well, saying how Keir wasn't happy about it so Doolan's killed him because Keir wouldn't grab the drugs. Telling a story about how Doolan was the one pushing for the information from her, he wouldn't just take photographs. Says he threatened her unless she came with information for things he could put aside.

Atlanta with her broad shoulders and all six feet of frame, walks off, to stand looking out into the darkness while her two goons keep guns trained on the kneeling pair. Doolan starts to cry but Atlanta tells him to shut it.

I can see him panic and when the gun's put to his head, he soils himself. It would be easy to sit and watch the drama and that's what Susan's doing until I nudge her. I'm counting two goons plus Atlanta but I'm thinking there's going to be a driver in the car as well. So far tonight's been a success, the boys have been caught. The Police will trace the drop-off, but this is where it could all go wrong. I said I'd get Leah out and I need to, but I also want the police here to catch this in action, it's better than anything I could have made up. I was going to leave stories on bits of paper and that to pull Doolan in on the drugs but here, he's smack in the middle of it.

I make my way around to the car, the black one that's sitting at the front of the house, with the driver standing outside. He's obviously been told to keep guard but he's not holding a weapon, just leaning casually in against the car. I creep up almost in front of him, but he can't see me in the dark. It takes a long time to get this good and that's why I've left Susan where she is. I come up from the rear side of him, I'm going to get one shot at this, and I reach up before quickly throwing my arm, my hand grabbing his face and bouncing his head off the car.

It's quite a blow and I can see the lights go out on his face quickly. In the rain, he never heard me approach. As he hits the ground, I place another kick across his jaw to make sure he's out. He's certainly not moving. With that, I place a 999-call

CHAPTER TWENTY-ONE

saying there's a disturbance with guns at the Doolan's house, so they'll come running. I make my way quickly back but as I'm only halfway there, I hear the gunshot.

My heart sinks, I didn't honestly think she'd do it, I thought she'd put them in the car and go. Racing back to Susan to make sure she's okay I find her struggling, trying to hold herself together at what she's just seen. Doolan's on the ground, well, there's parts of him elsewhere as well and Atlanta is now standing holding a gun on Leah's head and she tells the boys beside her to go to the car, she wants to do this properly. They start to walk off and I know I haven't got long. She's telling Leah to get to her feet which Leah does and then Atlanta bends down, kissing her on the lips, running her hands here and there. I guess it's one final goodbye. Her obsession with Leah is obviously great but business is business and she'll finish her off.

I haven't got a gun on me mainly because if I got caught tonight, the last thing I wanted to do was be standing holding a gun. When I say get caught, I mean by the police; there was never any intentions of getting caught by anybody else. But I know I have to move now, or Leah will be dead. On the ground, there's a sword, which was used for the shoot and it stands about the height of Leah, that's at least five foot three. It's some sort of broadsword, quite ornate. I don't think it's a claymore, but I have no idea what the weight of it will be. It's going to have to do. I'm approaching from behind Atlanta as she steps back, having kissed Leah for the last time. She's about to raise the gun and I run forward, put one hand on the sword handle, grabbing it and spin with all I've got. The sword comes round in an arc, and the flat of it strikes the back of Atlanta's head. She tumbles down, the gun falling from her hand, she's not out cold and starts to yell.

I try to kick at her, straight into her gut, and there are flashing blue lights all around. I hear yells from her boys, telling her the police are here. As they run to get into the car, I hear the engine start and they're shouting for their boss but she's on the ground now as I give her another couple of kicks. I point to Leah, indicating we have to go. She can't help herself and she gives a kick as well straight into Atlanta's face.

I grab Leah's hand and run straight towards Susan. You have to remember that although Leah's not well dressed, she is dressed in bright armour which clanks when she moves. Reaching Susan, I whisper for her to remove her jacket and start to peel the armour off Leah. It takes all of thirty seconds and she has a jacket thrown round her, zipped up the front and I'm holding her hand again, moving through the undergrowth. The car is miles away, which is good. It's sitting somewhere normal, in a roadside car park and it's going to stay there. It's under an anonymous name and on the front of it, there's a message saying 'gone hiking' so if they find it in the meantime it hopefully will be okay. But I'm going to walk a route that goes all round about it.

I can hear the dogs and wonder if they've got any scent. Dropping the armour may have been a bad idea because they can pick scent up from that. I told Maggie to have *Craigantlet* at Ulva ferry and we'd be there anytime from two onwards. That's quite a distance from where we are now but, in the car, it will take no time at all. On foot, it's going to be too long and have us too exposed in the open. We need to make a move quick before anything else is going on, before they realize that people are missing. We keep heading to the southwest corner, staying close to the road, but not so much as to be visible.

CHAPTER TWENTY-ONE

I come across a house and see a shed at the back. I casually break into it and inside are bikes which I take out, telling my companions to get on them. Leah is obviously scared for her life but something's pushing her on. She's dressed only in Susan's jacket and the rain's pouring off her cold skin, but this is a chance for freedom and she's going to take it. We race out onto the road, paddling as hard as we can. I can hear a car coming behind us and we turn off into a ditch, pulling the bikes down with us. It passes by and I don't know if it was a police car or just an ordinary one, but we get back up and pedal some more.

It takes us an hour but as we run up the road to Ulva ferry, we haven't seen a car for the last forty minutes. I can see the light of a boat in the distance. Maggie's moored around in the bay probably with the idea of coming to get us with her tender but as we cycle up to the pier side, I can see a car coming this direction. Hopefully, Maggie has the sense to stay inside. It'll be with us in a couple of minutes, so I tell my companions to take the bikes and throw them off the pier into the water.

Having watched them sink, we run off the pier and hide behind some rocks some distance on. I see uniformed officers get out, search around with lights, look out towards whatever boats are out there. They can see *Craigantlet* sitting with one anchor light on and no one on board. There's another boat further down, again, no one there. Another one tied up alongside. They search for a bit, then disappear. We strike out into the water, cold as it is for what's less than a ten-minute swim across.

Leah's not the strongest of swimmers but with Susan and I giving her assistance, we manage to get alongside *Craigantlet* and be pulled on board inside the tiny cabin. There's no space to worry about your decency and we strip off and get dried down before finding clothes for everyone inside the cabin. We do this all in the dark with only a small light on. The three of us then sit in front of the fire, the stove running slowly, and I look into it, hoping we've done all right. Maggie puts her arms around me and I feel her kiss on my neck.

'I bring a boat all the way to meet you in the middle of the night and you bring me my daughter soaking wet and a woman with just a coat on. You know how to impress a woman, don't you, Paddy Smythe?' I chuckled to myself and tell her to get underway—it's time to head south.

Chapter Twenty-Two

We sail through the night making our way down the coast before stopping off down at Portpatrick not far from Loch Ryan. Here, Martha steps ashore and comes back ten minutes later with a package under her arm. It's been quick work and I'm quite amazed at the passport. I've slept most of the journey down to here, Maggie coming in to wake me up and we continue to sail across the sea to Northern Ireland. In the dead of night, we take the tender ashore, dropping Martha and Leah off just outside Ballycastle.

Martha shakes my hand and I thank her, telling her as ever it's been a pleasure working with her and she really needs to take up that volleyball. Leah looks at me dressed in some of Susan's clothes. She starts to thank me and then bursts into tears. I nod, let her have a moment before Martha takes her away. I don't know where Martha's taking her, I don't know who they are meeting, and I don't know which country Leah's going to, but I don't care. She's safe and she's out of it.

She tried to tell me on the way over on *Craigantlet* about where she'd come from. I stopped Leah, told her to tell Martha. Then when she'd fallen asleep, Martha came and told me that Leah had been part of the trafficking ring in England and got moved up, having been spotted by Atlanta during an evening, and taken aside by her. The last three years Leah's been her companion, as Martha put it, although I think the word companion has a different meaning to me. Apparently, she has family somewhere, though again, Martha didn't tell me where, but she did say she would try and reunite Leah with them. And that's where I had to leave it.

I want to wrap up all the loose ends, make sure she gets to where she needs to be, but Martha does that. If anyone comes for me and God knows there could be plenty of people coming for me, I want to make sure that the people I helped aren't found by people they put away. We spend a couple of days on *Craigantlet* sailing in the north of Ireland, just getting away from it. During this time, I receive a phone call from Macleod telling me how the drug bust went slightly wrong and they found a dead man there. Seemingly, he was an informant. But someone was missing. Macleod wasn't sure but didn't believe they were not a player, but rather a pawn in the game having found a number of compromising photographs. The wife of the dead man can't believe he was involved in such things and said she had a private investigator.

He asks me if I know Sarah Hunstanton. I say I've met her before, because it's always best to be truthful but he said that she was off island and not around at the time. Sarah told him that she believed the man was having an affair and that's what she was sent in to look at. He asked how I got on with working out what happened to the young lad. I tell him it was cold case. I found the people he'd been working with, nobody knew anything, and I couldn't add to their investigation. The boys on the *Sandra Jane* haven't said a word either or Macleod would have been on to me. I guess they're scared but at least they might get a bit of protection now, not that I really care for

CHAPTER TWENTY-TWO

them either, just down to make fast cash, and didn't even come forward when Keir died, so stuff them.

The only person I truly feel sorry for is Annie Doolan. The woman was cheated on and then lost her husband but for the next two weeks, I'm putting that out of my mind and spending some quality time with Maggie and Susan.

Three months later after everything's died down, I take Keir's mother, Mrs. Matheson, to Gometra. It's a sombre moment as we cross on the Ulva ferry and in truth, for her age, the woman's strong and walks the whole way to Gometra with me. There's light rain and it's cold so I've brought a flask with me just so she can have some nice sweet warm tea when we get there. I point out where Keir died, I tell her exactly how he was found, which she already knows and then I leave her. She kneels down to the ground and cries.

When we leave Gometra, I take Mrs Matheson back on the ferry and then round to Calgary Bay explaining what had happened. I show her photographs of Leah but not the sort of ones where Leah has no clothes, or we cut them so it's a shoulders and head shot. I don't lie to the woman, tell his mother that Keir was infatuated with Leah and that he was doing his best to help her escape. There was a man who was also infatuated with Leah who killed Keir. In truth, it's such a waste and I explain to Mrs Matheson that the man's now dead. Sarah Hunstanton joins us and together we meet at Annie Doolan's and I take Annie and Sarah through what happened.

It's hard to decide if Annie's sad, heartbroken or just relieved it's all over. She tells me they were never that close, how she always felt there was this other side to him, a side to Jack Doolan that Annie didn't know. She finds it hard to believe that every time she was away, he was off photographing this woman.

Her hatred of Leah is dulled when I tell her Leah was trafficked, tell her that Jack was working with drug smugglers. Of course, I give no real names and it's all hearsay. Annie never gets my name other than Paddy. I'm just a colleague working for Sarah and it's all Sarah's case and hasn't she done remarkably well.

When I take Mrs. Matheson back and place her on a train in Oban back to her own home, I decide to return again. Maggie's with me and I leave Susan behind. I show Maggie the beaches that we came to, where these strange photography scenes were taking place and then go and sit on Calgary Bay. Today it's cold, the clouds are passing over, and that long winding beach is still ahead of us as we sit on the grass. From our position you can see the graveyard and then beyond it, the spot where the fresher graves were and where the drugs were hidden. There's a woman looking across the graveyard who then walks away past the other grave without barely a look. So much here was hidden under the surface. I take Maggie past the house where the drug smugglers were, and my hand feels the handcuff that I was hanging by and I explain to her how lucky we were with Susan.

She reiterates to me as she always does, that it's Susan's choice and then when I tell her about Hans, how it was his choice as well, I promise to one day introduce them so she can thank him properly for helping bring her daughter back.

'You did good, Paddy,' she says. 'That woman's at peace now. She understands what happened to her son and there's justice and a woman's free of a life of slavery.'

'I know all this,' I say, 'but Jack Doolan still died, and he died right in front of your Susan and what bothers me is that she hasn't spoken of it yet.'

'She will, Paddy, she definitely will, and we'll be there for her like I'm here for you now.'

    We sit for two hours, her arms around my neck, occasionally sipping on our tea. The clouds pass overhead, threatening rain but never coming while the sea rolls up the bay taking away some of the sand. It's funny how in some of the most beautiful spots in the world you can't see what's hidden away and part of me gets a chill because I realize my job is to expose this.

Get Your Patrick Smythe Series Short Story!

GET YOUR PATRICK SMYTHE SERIES SHORT STORY!

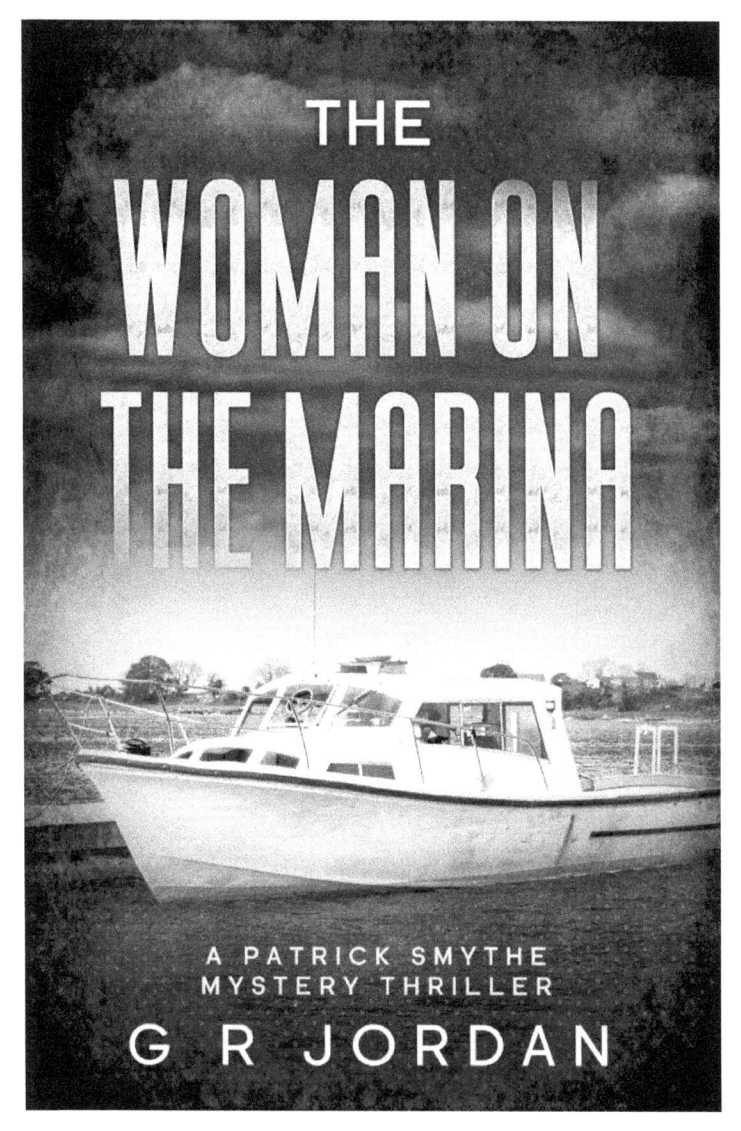

Get the Patrick Smythe short story here!

Patrick Smythe is a former Northern Irish policeman who after suffering an amputation after a bomb blast, takes to the sea between the west coast of Scotland and his homeland to ply his trade as a private investigator. Join Paddy as he tries to work to his own ethics while knowing how to bend the rules he once enforced. Working from his beloved motorboat 'Craigantlet', Paddy decides to rescue a drug mule in this short story from the pen of G R Jordan.

Join G R Jordan's monthly newsletter about forthcoming releases and special writings for his tribe of avid readers and then receive your free Patrick Smythe short story.

Go to *https://bit.ly/PatrickSmythe* for your Patrick Smythe journey to start!

About the Author

GR Jordan is a self-published author who finally decided at forty that in order to have an enjoyable lifestyle, his creative beast within would have to be unleashed. His books mirror that conflict in life where acts of decency contend with self-promotion, goodness stares in horror at evil, and kindness blindsides us when we at our worst. Corrupting our world with his parade of wondrous and horrific characters, he highlights everyday tensions with fresh eyes whilst taking his methodical, intelligent mainstays on a roller-coaster ride of dilemmas, all the while suffering the banter of their provocative sidekicks.

A graduate of Loughborough University where he masqueraded as a chemical engineer but ultimately played American football, Gary had worked at changing the shape of cereal flakes and pulled a pallet truck for a living. Watching vegetables freeze at -40'C was another career highlight and he was also one of the Scottish Highlands "blind" air traffic controllers. These days he has graduated to answering a telephone to people in trouble before telephoning other people to sort it out.

Having flirted with most places in the UK, he is now based in the Isle of Lewis in Scotland where his free time is spent between raising a young family with his wife, writing, figuring out how to work a loom and caring for a small flock of chickens. Luckily, his writing is influenced by his varied work and life experience as the chickens have not been the poetical inspiration he had hoped for!

You can connect with me on:
- https://grjordan.com
- https://facebook.com/carpetlessleprechaun

Subscribe to my newsletter:
- https://bit.ly/PatrickSmythe

Also by G R Jordan

G R Jordan writes across multiple genres including crime, dark and action adventure fantasy, feel good fantasy, mystery thriller and horror fantasy. Below is a selection of his work in the crime and islands genres. Whilst all books are available across online stores, signed copies are available at his personal shop.

The Fairy Pools' Gathering (Patrick Smythe Book 3)
A desperate woman fears her husband's sudden change. Men in white perform ceremonies in the dark. Can Paddy unmask the terror that's putting businesses to the sword?

When Patrick Smythe is asked to investigate a woman's plea about a man's mid-life crisis, he sends his young partner to an easy mark. But when a local tourist site becomes the scene for strange meetings and intimidation, Paddy and Susan are drawn into the underworld of the local tourist industry.

'The Fairy Pools' Gathering' is the third full Patrick Smythe adventure involving the Ulster native and one-armed investigator with a knack for finding dangerous situations amidst lies and deceit. If you love fast-paced action and an underdog to root for, Patrick Smythe will fly all your kites.

It's all smoke and mirrors until someone gets hurt!

The Disappearance of Russell Hadleigh (Patrick Smythe Book 1)

A retired judge fails to meet his golf partner. His wife calls for help while running a fantasy play ring. When Russians start co-opting into a fairly-traded clothing brand, can Paddy untangle the strands before the bodies start littering the golf course?

In his first full novel, Patrick Smythe, the single-armed former policeman, must infiltrate the golfing social scene to discover the fate of his client's husband. Assisted by a young starlet of the greens, Paddy tries to understand just who bears a grudge and who likes to play in the rough, culminating in a high stakes showdown where lives are hanging by the reaction of a moment. If you love pacey action, suspicious motives and devious characters, then Paddy Smythe operates amongst your kind of people.

Love is a matter of taste but money always demands more of its suitor.

The Pirate Club: A Highlands and Islands Detective Thriller (Highlands & Islands Detective Book 6)

A body holding a spade in the sand amidst tales of a missing gem. An old boy's network whose members are rapidly becoming extinct. Can Macleod solve the gamester's clues before the club players are liquidated and the prize is gone forever?

In the sixth major case of Macleod and McGrath's partnership, a deadly game is being played in the search for a long-stolen jewel of fantastic wealth. Whilst former friends dispatch their new enemies, DI Macleod hunts the pieces of parchment that will lead him to the resting place of a Sultan's pride and joy, and the killers who cannot live without it. Will the pirate king emerge triumphant, or can the Inspector run their plans asunder?

When precious things seem out of reach, death may be the only compromise.

Highlands and Islands Detective Thriller Series
Join stalwart DI Macleod and his burgeoning new female DC McGrath as they look into the darker side of the stunningly scenic and wilder parts of the north of Scotland.

From the Black Isle to Lewis, Mull to Harris and across to the small Isles, the Uists and Barra, this mismatched pairing follow murders, thieves and vengeful victims in an effort to restore tranquillity to the remoter parts of the land.

Join this tale of a surprise partnership amidst the foulest deeds and darkest souls who stalk this peaceful and most beautiful of lands, and you'll never see the Highlands the same way again.

Surface Tensions (Island Adventures Book 1)

Mermaids sighted near a Scottish island. A town exploding in anger and distrust. And Donald's got to get the sexiest fish in town, back in the water.

"Surface Tensions" is the first story in a series of Island adventures from the pen of G R Jordan. If you love comic moments, cosy adventures and light fantasy action, then you'll love these tales with a twist. Get the book that amazon readers said, "perfectly captures life in the Scottish Hebrides" and that explores "human nature at its best and worst".

Something's stirring the water!

Milton Keynes UK
Ingram Content Group UK Ltd.
UKHW041404041224
3408UKWH00027B/92

9 781912 153763